NEWTOWN CREEK

J C GRAEME

TANIWHA PRESS UK

0

Published by the Taniwha Press UK

All rights reserved. No part of this publication may be reproduced, transmitted or used in any form by any means - graphic, electronic or mechanical, including photocopying, recording, taping or information storage and retrieval systems or otherwise - without the prior permission of the Publishers.

© Rod Heikell writing as J.C.Graeme 2024. Rod Heikell has asserted his right under the Copyright, Designs and Patents Act 1988 to be identified as the author of this work.

British Library Cataloguing in Publication Data
Graeme, J.C.

Title   Newtown Creek
Type   Fiction. Novel
1st edition 2024
ISBN   978-1-7397072-4-8

A bit of an explanation.

From *The Mapmaker's Shadow*. In the first two novels I wrote, *To Ithaca* and *My Name is No One*, I used the moniker J C Graeme as a pen name. That might seem a bit unnecessary but at the time I had been critically ill with tuberculosis and I really wanted to be someone else. I'm sure I'm not alone in wanting to be someone new, someone whose life I could step into and play-act at. So, I created J C Graeme. The J C was my father's first two initials: John Charles. Graeme was my late brother's middle name. Magically J C Graeme came into being, an imaginary friend and at times an annoying homunculus carping at the injustices of the world. I still like him though. **Rod Heikell**

The original bio: J C Graeme

J C Graeme is a retired history teacher who has spent thirty years sailing his own small boat, *Apagio*, around the Mediterranean. He has written several books on the history of the Mediterranean. His knowledge of both the sea itself and its history is unrivalled. His first novel was *To Ithaca*. His second novel, *My Name is No One*, is a wry reworking of the *Odyssey* as told in Homer's Sunset Bar on Khios. His last novel before this was *The Mapmaker's Shadow*. When he is not sailing, he lives in Douarnenez in Brittany with his Jack Russell *Odysseus*.

My thanks as always to Lucinda, my wife, who patiently (most of the time) puts up with me straying into other worlds.

There is a tide in the affairs of men, Which taken at the flood, leads on to fortune. Omitted, all the voyage of their life is bound in shallows and in miseries. On such a full sea are we now afloat. And we must take the current when it serves, or lose our ventures.

Julius Caesar   William Shakespeare

EM'S STORY
SHAPED BY THE SEA

i

Em ran the sander over the turn of the hull one last time before running his hand over it to check it was as smooth as it looked to his eye. He stood back and followed the curve of the forefoot down to the keel, a shape for water sculpted by the designer to gladden the eye of the casual observer as much as to slice cleanly through old mother sea. He put the sander down and coughed again to clear the dust from his throat.

'Em. You still here?' It was Mick, the owner of the little boatyard on the Medina River that Em rented space from. Still rented space. He had been three years building this boat and Mick often chided him for the time and detail Em put into it – in a kind way. Still, most of these Lyle Hess designs were works of art, many of them built by semi-amateur builders that learned the dark art of wooden boatbuilding as they went along. Em was proud of his acquired skills learned while building the boat.

Em coughed into his hand again and looked at the little specks of blood in his palm. 'I wish you would wear a mask', Mick said. 'That teak dust isn't good for you let alone all the other resins and stuff you have been using.'
Em grinned at him. 'I know dad', he said, 'But nag, nag, nag. It will wash out.' Mick was younger than him, another one of those who had washed up on the island and stayed. His New Zealand accent was less broad now, but still obvious.

Washed up here just like he had, Em thought. How long now? Must be at least fifteen years or more now since he had arrived on the island, the young cocky helm of Bridgewater's yacht *East Street*. He looked at his thirty foot Hess design based on the Falmouth Quay punts of a hundred years ago, at the old fashioned lines and long keel, at the gleaming brightwork and the dull contrasting grey of the teak, and couldn't help but think this wooden creation was a million miles away from the carbon fibre racing yachts he once sailed on these waters. A million miles away from the back-slapping and red trousers of the Squadron and the other royal yacht clubs in Cowes. He had never been comfortable there.

'Want that beer?' Mick asked him. Em nodded and the two of them trooped out to the concrete quay on the river. Two battered plastic chairs were perched against the yard shed and Mick disappeared into his ramshackle office and returned with two cans of beer. The two of them sat silently in the evening sun looking out over the Medina. The odd yacht motored by punching up the river. Em rolled a cigarette and offered one to Mick. Neither of them was a big talker and they were content to sit in silence for much of the time watching the wind on the water rucking up a short chop against the ebb.

Eventually Mick popped the question that always came up. 'So how long before you finish the boat Em? I'm not complaining but you are a bit behind in the yard bills. And have you got a name for the boat yet?'

Em nodded. 'Should be only another month or so before she goes in the water' he replied. He knew Mick wasn't going to kick him out but he did wonder how to get the money together to settle up. Mick was a good friend, but he knew that he shouldn't be taking advantage of him. Goddamn, if he had the money he would have paid. And more. He thought back to the old glory days skippering *East Street* and how then he had more than enough in the bank to settle the yard bill and plenty left over.

ii

Em was a bit of a mystery to most people but Mick knew most of the story from back in the day, well everyone did really, and like many others, he had harboured suspicions about Bridgewater and his sudden appearance on the yachting scene. When it came out the papers were full of it. Mick thought back over the whole affair, an affair that had made headline news in the Daily's and had been the subject of endless conversations by sailors around the world.

Practically every bar had a buzz of conversation that mentioned Bridgewater and by association, Em's name.

That name was Emile James Jefferson, born into a single parent family in the wastelands of Essex. He always hated the name Emile, from a grandfather he never met, so at school shortened it to Em. Not that it stopped the other kids ragging him. His was a rags to riches, or at least rags to fame story, that had occupied a lot of column inches in the press at the time. Em had little to say about himself to the press but he did have a mother who loved to put more make-up on than was needed and who often appeared to be somewhat the worse for wear and verbing her slurs on camera. It was a media circus, though the only performer who was missing was Em.

Em had been taken under the wing of one of the teachers at his school who persuaded him to try out on one of the school fleet of Optimists. He quickly worked his way up through the dinghy classes until he got to the Finn. He wasn't at home with the other snotty-nosed kids who raced dinghies, but he had some natural talent and a stubborn competitive streak. Em had to be in front of the fleet. When he won the Finn nationals and then the European championships, people started to take notice. He might not be a member of a posh sailing club but he could sail and keep on winning and it was unsurprising that he was soon employed as boat captain and then skipper on a racing yacht in the Solent.

Em took the leap from dinghies to a full-blown racing yacht in his stride. Of the owners with yachts racing out of Cowes, there was one man who took a particular interest and that was Stephen Bridgewater, the real estate and media mogul who had interests in the UK and the USA and a casual interest in fast sailing boats.

Bridgewater recognised something of himself in Em. He came from the same poor background as Em. In fact, he had grown up just a few miles away from Em's high rise flat on the Dagenham estate. Bridgewater had left school at fifteen and worked on a stall in Walworth Market selling second-hand books and stationery. He soon found out the stall owner did more business in 'top-shelf' magazines than he ever did selling old paperbacks. Bridgewater soon had his own stall and with the contacts he had acquired stocked a busy top-shelf selling everything from heavy sadomasochism to homoerotica for the boys and girls. He acquired another stall in East Street nearer home and built a reputation for being able to get his hands on anything that customers asked for.

While Bridgewater was making good money from his magazines, he also had bigger ambitions for the trade. In the market, he met a photographer who seemed perpetually wreathed in cigarette smoke and the whiff of whiskey. He had complained about how work had dried up so Bridgewater took him on, rented an apartment, and set up a photographic studio to produce his own magazines.

Bridgewater had a canny eye for assessing the needs of his customers and he spent a good deal of money setting up the studio to look like an opulent country house. He had velvet drapes, big wingback armchairs and a damask Ottoman with plump satin cushions sitting on an old Persian carpet. A large tapestry showing satyrs hunting in the forest formed the backdrop. Silver bowls had fruit overflowing onto the floor and goblets of wine placed haphazardly around the set.

Grigsby, the photographer, was a wonder. Before the booze, he had owned a well-known studio in Soho taking photos of celebrities and when he was in the mood he could light the makeshift studio to look a good deal more opulent than even Bridgewater had imagined for his photoshoots. Bridgewater promised the young girls around the estate a chance to do shoots for prospective modelling assignments. If they showed promise he offered to pay them for what he called 'posh nude assignments' and the chance to make good money from the big magazines. Given the life chances of most of the applicants was to aspire to a job in the local fast food outlet or to work in one of the supermarkets, Bridgewater was not surprised at how many of them queued up for a shot at some sort of fame.

If he was nothing else Bridgewater was ambitious. His soft porn with the 'country house' look sold well and after a year Bridgewater decided to buy the small printing works that produced his magazines. When the local newspaper, the *Barking Gazette*, was about to go under, Bridgewater bought it out and revamped it so it had spicier stories than its stale predecessor. By the time he was thirty Bridgewater had a small media empire and a not-so-small porn publishing business. He had also realised the value of real estate so he started buying houses in areas where no one else wanted them but which could command rents high enough to repay the bank and make a modest profit.

iii

It was on a jolly in Cowes where his lawyer had invited him out on a friend's yacht that Bridgewater got hooked on the sailing scene. He could see that mixing with the slacks and blazer brigade conveyed a status he had not found anywhere else and in some strange way, he enjoyed being out on the water with the yacht cutting through the waves under sail. He enjoyed lording it over drinks on board after a race. He made a few inquiries and decided to commission a yacht to race in the Admirals' cup.

Not knowing anything about the sport he asked around, got a few recommendations, and hired a skipper and crew to race his new yacht. *East Street* was a revolutionary design by an up and coming New Zealand naval architect and Bridgewater was happy to spend money on the project and crew.

Although he craved recognition and kudos from the self-important men of the blazers and red trousers corps, he was still not overly comfortable in their company. He wanted to win and with that in mind scouted around for a new skipper. That was when he came across Em fresh from his European triumphs and skippering a yacht for one of the highfalutin' members of a royal yacht club. He offered him double what he was getting and so Em became skipper of *East Street*.

The papers had colourful details of the glory years of the barrow-boy-made-good story bringing a touch of Essex to the plummy cadre in Cowes. *East Street* had been the winning boat in the Admiral's Cup under Em and gone on to gather a string of cups in regattas around the world. Bridgewater made sure no one doubted who was behind the campaign and the Squadron reluctantly invited Bridgewater in. There were even rumours that Bridgewater would mount an America's Cup campaign and that Em would drive the boat.

Bridgewater was not quite ready for the tens of millions of dollars an America's Cup campaign cost, but he was enamoured of the recognition his *East Street* campaign had fired up and he was hungry for more recognition and respect amongst the Squadron set at Cowes. While he had gained an entrée into the ranks of the titled and entitled world of yacht racing, he craved more. By this time Bridgewater had expanded his media empire and bought up a number of heavyweight daily papers and a few magazines as well. And then he made a major move and bought a start-up satellite television company that had been bleeding money ever since it started. Without anyone noticing, or so it seemed, Bridgewater had become a big player in the media world.

Em was not unaware of all these goings-on, but he had little interest in them. After all, his company credit card worked and his salary was paid. What had interested him from the early days was skippering the boat and winning.

Em was like the son Bridgewater never had and so it was inevitable he often invited him to the new family holiday house in Gurnard on the island. As Em stacked up more wins on *East Street* Bridgewater was determined to make an even bigger splash on the yachting scene. He installed Em in an apartment on the waterfront in Cowes and began talking about building a new yacht.

'Been thinking about where to go with this yachting business. What I want to do is build a new boat but for the maxi-series. I want you to oversee the build and run the campaign. We will base it here in Cowes – probably build it here or close by. It's to be a race boat but with some mod cons for cruising the damn thing. After all these boats cost a small fortune. But you can choose somewhere else if it can be done there as well and, yeah, maybe cheaper. Always look for the deal I say. And who knows where this might lead eh?'

Em nodded dumbly. This was all news to him. Though he knew Bridgewater was doing well he hadn't expected him to splash out like this. It wasn't in his nature. But then again he was happy in his flashy apartment Bridgewater provided and he had more money in the bank than he needed. He kept himself busy talking to designers, yacht builders and organising the sort of crew he wanted for a big boat campaign.

iv

Bridgewater was often in Cowes with his wife and two daughters. His wife was a determined blond with a penchant for diaphanous dresses and high heels. Em often had to remonstrate with her to take the high heels off before stepping on board. She would pout and reluctantly discard them on the pontoon. Em was not someone to be messed with. The younger daughter Chloe was a carbon copy of her mother except for the more or less natural hair colour. The older daughter Sophie was the polar opposite of the two of them: unruly mad chestnut hair and a dress sense of whatever first came out of a pile of clothes.

Sophie disliked the shopping tours her mother and Chloe were so fond of and in Cowes would frequent the waterfront and marinas along the banks of the Medina. When she approached Em to be part of the crew on *East Street* he was nonplussed and could only mutter that she could try out as ballast, as a rail rat. He never expected her to last long. Sophie turned out to be a quick learner and could more than cope with the rough and tumble of life on board the boat. She never used the fact that her father owned the boat to work her way from rail rat to learning the ropes and soon was doing the foredeck and in charge of the spinnaker hoist. Em was quietly impressed.

After practice out on the Solent she would often sit with Em and the others, all male, grilling them on how everything worked on the boat. She had the earthy directness of her father but none of the darkness. It was probably inevitable that Em and Sophie would tumble into bed together at some point.

It happened after a club race around the buoys when Sophie stayed on at Em's flat after the others had left, talking to him about his past life. This was not something Em would usually talk about, but somehow over a second bottle of Sauvignon Blanc he told Sophie about his upbringing on the estate, about his mother, about his outlook on life as an outsider.

Sophie was overwhelmed and had tears in her eyes as Em recounted his history. He put his arm around her to comfort her saying it was all past history, inconsequential, not anything to worry about these days. The next minute she was kissing him and stroking his hair and he hers. He led her into the bedroom and pulled the covers over Sophie and his old history.

It didn't take long before Sophie moved in with Em. He wasn't sure what her father thought of this but there was nothing said overtly from him and just a curt nod when he saw them together. He delighted in her company and for the first time in his life felt good about himself, about the world around him, about all the little niggles he had with what he was doing.

Sophie turned out to be a good cook and amused him with all sorts of cuisine he had never tried before mixing Mediterranean and Asian flavours, serving up old English favourites with a French twist, slow cooking Indian curries that tasted so much better than the standard takeaways he normally ordered.

On *East Street* she soon took over the running of the boat organising crew interviews, gear updates, provisioning, sorting out any complaints and generally trying to keep everyone, including Em, happy. She was good at it and apart from a few uppity nobs who tried to trip her up on who did what on the boat, the majority of the crew were happy with what she was doing. If not she would see them off *East Street*. While Bridgewater kept a firm grip on the finances of his little empire, with *East Street* he was more than happy to let Sophie have a free rein.

V

For a while Em heard nothing more from Bridgewater about the plans for a new boat. Several years went by and it suited him as he didn't want too much distraction from his new-found life on the island with Sophie and his continued success with *East Street*. He had heard a few whispers about problems with Bridgewater's empire, but here on the island he had little interest in Bridgewater's businesses or the rumours circulating around them.

It was Sophie who raised the subject with Em. 'You do know what Dad is doing - don't you?

You do know where much of his money comes from?' she asked him after dinner one night. Em nodded and mumbled something about real estate and communications companies and newspapers and such. He didn't really have any in depth knowledge of the workings of Bridgewater's companies. 'Yes, it's that and other stuff. He made his initial fortune in porn and a lot of his companies are still a front for porn as well. Yes, he does straight stuff though he is leveraged to the sky with most of his acquisitions, but he still makes lots of his money from porn of one sort or another: magazines, online web sites, even the pin-up girls in the newspapers are groomed by him for this backroom little industry of his.'

Em grunted in surprise and looked shifty as Sophie kept her gaze on him. 'I don't really take that much interest in that', he said. 'I just go sailing for him and win races. That seems to keep him happy.'
Sophie looked disdainfully at him. 'You should worry. I do. And I find it difficult to live with that knowledge while he plies all and sundry with champagne and bonhomie. It's built on shifting

sand and exploitation and you know what? It stinks. I'm going to have it out with him. Tell him what I think. I don't care if he disowns me. I'd rather work as a waitress or something, anything that's clean and without the smell of corrupt business.'

Em looked stunned. He could see his world falling apart, his job as race captain on *East Street* disappearing, this life on the island crumbling away. He looked angrily at Sophie. 'Alright for you', he muttered. 'But what about me, what about us, what would we do? I really think we should sit on this and think about what our future might be. I'm not convinced you would survive for long as a waitress in some greasy café.' Sophie looked back bitterly at him. 'Maybe', she muttered looking away. 'Or, maybe you don't know me well enough.'

She didn't sleep with him that night, choosing the spare bed in the other bedroom.

vi

The argument between Em and Sophie led to both of them living a life as if the other wasn't there. They edged around one another and found things to occupy themselves with that kept them out of each other's way. Em kept himself to himself, he always had, but still he hurt inside with the distance between them. He had been happy before, yes happy he thought to himself, comfortable and comforted. His thoughts drifted back to his old life growing up in the council flat in Dagenham and he realised that he really didn't want to go back to that, to the taunting of his peer group, to the threat of the gangs in his neighbourhood, to life without much direction.

He realised he had got used to this pampered life on the island and to the crew around him on the yacht and on land. And especially to Sophie. He missed the intimacy of her snuggling into his back in bed and the easy familiarity between them. He hoped their problem could be resolved somehow and they could return to the old life they had.

Much as he missed the companionship and easy familiarity of his life with Sophie, he also couldn't help but feel some anger towards her. How would she know what it was like to go back to a council flat and scraping along when she had such a pampered upbringing? What did she know of scrimping and saving for small luxuries? He resented her refusal to leave this good life alone and just turn a blind eye to what Bridgewater did. They had a nice flat overlooking the Solent, a winning boat and the possibility of Bridgewater funding a maxi yacht. That excited him.

Despite their distance Sophie too wanted that old familiarity. The old comfort of the life before her argument with Em. She didn't understand how Em couldn't see the guilt she carried around and how she so wanted to rip it out of her life. Somewhere in her dreams she lived in a cottage on a smallholding with Em. They had a vegetable patch and dogs and a few sheep. A small orchard. This arcadian dream world outside of the grubby world of her father kept her safe. And Em was part of it. Or had been.

Mostly Sophie kept these dreams to herself except when Freddy came down to the marina. She called Freddy the pie-man, not in a derogatory way, but more an affectionate nickname because he made superb pies for crew lunches amongst other things. He had a small business called Freddy's Posh Nosh that supplied readymade food of all types for the yachts in Cowes. She had met him when he was first getting the business off the ground and had warmed to him straight away. There was something captivating about his cheeky enthusiasm to supply quality crew meals a bit out of the ordinary for the boats cruising and racing out of Cowes.

East Street was laid up at the end of that season and safely tied up in Shephard's Marina. At odd times Em went down to check on her and to do odd boat jobs. So did Sophie though she tended to avoid going on the boat when Em was there. They said tentative hellos to each other but little else until Sophie needed a hand one day to mouse the halyards on the boat and asked Em if he could help her. He grunted an affirmative and cycled down to the boat with her. Together they got the halyards out and moused and somehow, with this working together, they started talking again. It was a start, even if a hesitant one.

vii

Sophie realised that her anger and disdain at what her father did to earn the money she was brought up on was digging a pit in her soul. She decided she had to have it out with him and to make public who he was. It seemed like a betrayal but she wondered whether not doing so would be a betrayal to herself. And she needed to expel the anger she felt at being trapped between her father and the person she wanted to be.

Storm Alice was the remnants of a late season hurricane in the Atlantic and the first named storm of the winter. The news was continuously broadcasting warnings of hurricane strength winds along the south coast and that included the island. Em and Sophie went down to the marina and doubled up the lines on *East Street* and removed any loose items from the deck. Then they retreated to the apartment to wait for the inbound storm.

Alice arrived with a blast of rain and lightning arcing down onto the island. The wind threatened to implode the large windows of the apartment overlooking the Solent and Em was worried about how to repair them if they were pushed in by the violence of the wind. He hardly noticed Sophie leave and it took him a little while to see her scribbled note to him.

Em. You stay here to check on the house. I'm just down to East Street to check up on her. Don't worry – I'll be careful. Sophie.

When Em found the note he immediately ran down the stairs and hopped on his bike to get to *East Street*. It was blowing a hooley and waves were smashing up over the Esplanade onto the road. He didn't care and cycled furiously to the marina through the wind and spray.

When he arrived at the marina Em looked out over the cloud of spray and the waves breaking over the pontoon to where *East Street* was moored. It was difficult to see much through the wind driven rain and spray so he ventured down onto the pontoon and along the slippery boards to the boats moored there. He hoped Sophie wasn't here in this stormy tempest where the sea was being blown over the boats and it was difficult to stand in the wind. He got to the boat and saw nothing. Out of the corner of eye he thought he saw someone else on the pontoon further along but he couldn't be sure.

Then he noticed the red wet weather jacket floating in the water. Not just floating but attached to a body. He realised in horror it was Sophie's jacket and that it was Sophie floating face down in the water. He stripped off his own jacket and dived into the water. He found her and lifted her head above the water screaming to the sky for help. Someone must have heard him and as he paddled over to the pontoon with Sophie willing hands pulled them from the water and up onto the pontoon. He screamed for them to get an ambulance and began giving her mouth to mouth. He was still cradling Sophie's head and giving her mouth to mouth when the gentle hands of a paramedic lifted him away and started pumping her chest. Another paramedic arrived with a mobile stretcher and they put her on it and carried it up to an ambulance. Em sat exhausted on the pontoon until the police arrived.

Em staggered up to the quay and the yard with one of the policemen helping him. He was shivering by now and they took him into the office and rubbed him down with towels.
'Where is she' he rasped. His throat was burning from the saltwater.

'Were you with her when it happened?' one of the policemen asked him.
Em shook his head. 'She came down to check on the boat' he replied. 'She was on her own.' He groaned and went to get up. 'I need to go with her' he said, 'I need to be there.'

'She is in good hands' the policeman said. 'But we need a few details from you.'

Em gave them names, their address, phone numbers. The policeman advised him not to leave the island and then offered to give him a lift to the hospital. On the way his radio pinged him and he pulled over to the side of the road. Em couldn't hear most of the conversation but he did notice the grave expression on the policeman's face and the way he kept looking across to him. The policeman put the mike back on the radio and turned to Em.

'Listen Mr. Em. My name is Mark. I'm afraid I've got bad news for you.' Mark grimaced. 'Your wife... your partner, has passed I'm afraid. She was possibly already dead when you went into the water. The coroner will determine the cause of death. Meanwhile, I'll take you to the hospital and then home. The new flats on the waterfront I recall. You will need to come down to the station at some time, but not now. I'm very sorry.'

Em sat there for a moment. He felt numbed and lost. Sophie had been a touchstone for him, a little bit of love in a world that had seemed bereft of it. He nodded dumbly and gave Mark his address again.

viii

Bridgewater drove over the next day. He seemed unduly subdued over the news of his daughter's death and moreover avoided contact with Em. By this time Em had been interviewed down at the police station and cautioned not to leave the island. Somehow the papers had got hold of the story, likely through Bridgewater and his newspaper outlets, so Em's name was all over the media. It soon emerged that Sophie had bruise marks on her neck and a bruise on the back of the head. Em was the number one suspect and Bridgewater soon found this out. He ordered Em out of the flat and told him he would do all he could to put scum like him behind bars for life. He had a malevolence to him that Em had only suspected before and so he moved onto a friend's yacht in the marina on the other side of the Medina River while the police investigated the death of Sophie.

Somehow the reporters found him after a week or so and harassed him so that he had to run a gauntlet of cameras and men shouting questions at him. He moved again to a chalet in the holiday park in Gurnard but they found him there too. By now the police had opened a homicide inquiry.

The police soon established that while Em had motive, notably the estrangement between Em and Sophie, he could not be placed on the pontoon around the time of the homicide though he was there shortly after. He was the only person about when Sophie was presumed to have drowned. The purely circumstantial evidence didn't stop the reporters from conducting a trial by newsprint that found him guilty. You could see the hand of Bridgewater directing the news agenda and although Em was never brought to trial, he was effectively convicted and found guilty as far as the press was concerned.

ix

He first heard about it from a friend who phoned him up. 'Em. Have you seen the papers? You need to take a look pronto. Your boss, sorry your ex-boss, is in big trouble.'

'Give me a clue Ian. What's going on?' Em was at a loss to know what was up with Bridgewater. Nothing he had heard of.

'It's a bit of scandal' Ian replied. 'Something about bankruptcy and stuff coming out about some porn empire he is involved in.'
Em turned on the television to the news channel. Sure enough, there was a picture of Bridgewater up on the screen and a reporter talking about the collapse of Bridgewater's companies. There was more on the uncovering of a porn ring that Bridgewater owned through one of his offshore companies and which had come to light when his various other companies had gone belly up.

Although it was patently clear that Em had nothing to do with Bridgewater's companies or his porn empire, somehow Em was tainted by the whole affair. He was universally rebuffed for skippering jobs and ignored by owners. There was little doubt that the collapse of Bridgewater's companies and the exposure of his porn empire were quietly celebrated by the denizens of the Squadron and other royal yacht clubs around Cowes. Bridgewater had been tolerated for his money and not for his presence. Em had been accepted as his skipper and a grudging respect for his talent. No more. The slacks and blazer brigade would quickly forget about Bridgewater and his soiled new money.

Through a mate, Em found an old Beneteau 36 for sale in Southampton and got his mate to buy it for him and provision it up before bringing it over to the Medina River. The police had given him his passport back and one dark night he slipped away and sailed down channel. He wasn't sure where he was going, just that he had to go or they might find him floating face down in the water.

X

Em spent the next few years holed up in the Mediterranean. He delivered boats around the Med and across to the Caribbean for a hand-to-mouth living and pretty much kept himself to himself. Whenever he was recognised Em would up-anchor and move on. He left no records and only used cash. Although he had never got on with his mother, especially after the death of Sophie and her subsequent appearances on the media, he still had a nagging guilt that she might, just might, be concerned over his absence after the media scrum over Sophie's death. After his time away in the Med he provisioned up the boat and headed back to England to see her before he disappeared again.

He cleared in at Southampton and left the boat in Quayside up the River Itchen. He figured he was less likely to meet anyone he knew there though he doubted there would be anyone around after his absence. Em phoned the old number for his mother but only got a disconnected signal. That night he caught the train up to London and a taxi over to Dagenham. He felt like an intruder creeping around the old locale he had grown up in – familiar in its bleak aspect but also like a strange urban landscape he was not part of. He got to the block of flats where his mother lived and climbed the stairs to number 34.

Somehow he was not surprised when a stranger opened the door. Em asked him if he knew Mrs. Jefferson. 'Mrs. Jefferson, you say. Nah. Maybe number 32 knows. She been here the longest.' The man closed the door looking at Em suspiciously. He went down to 32 and knocked on the door there. He vaguely remembered that a Mrs. Bately had lived there and was surprised when a lined little face peered around the door and magically lit up with a giant smile.

'I knew you would finally come back here. Come in Emile.' She was fumbling with the various chains that prevented the door from opening wide, finally getting the last one off and opening the door, gesturing to him to come inside. She hobbled down the hall to the living room and pointed to an armchair. 'Sit. Sit Emile. You look older but still the same odd boy you always were. Your mother always said you were an odd one.'

Em nodded. 'Where is she?'

The old lady's eyes misted over. 'You don't know. Oh, poor boy. Your mother passed on, oh, three or more years ago. A cancer.'

He looked at her bleakly and nodded. The thought had crossed his mind she might not be alive, but he had always pushed the thought into a far corner in his head. Just as he had pushed away most of his past, so he had cleared any visions he might have of the future and concentrated on day-to-day tasks that kept him going through the day.
They had tea together and then the old lady told him she had something for him. She went into the next room and came back with a large envelope. Inside were several envelopes of letters addressed to him. 'These were from your mother's flat' Mrs. Bately said, 'Your mother said to keep them for you. Open them later.'

He travelled back down to Southampton and sailed the boat across to Cowes. Somehow he felt the time away had insulated him from everything that had happened on the island, that this was a new start and he could shuck off his old husk of a life and live here in some simple private way. He wondered if his old friend Mick still had his boatyard on the Medina and headed there first. Mick's face said it all as he gestured to Em to tie up on the stubby pontoon. Then he sat down for a beer with his old mate.

On York Street just off Cowes High Street, he rented a narrow terraced house and prepared to live on land once again. He was surprised no one seemed to want to bother him though he had to admit the sea and wind had creased his face and his hair was peppered with grey so he looked older and more careworn than he had when he left the island. If there were those who recognised him they left him pretty much alone.

Once he was settled into the house he remembered the letters Mrs. Bately had given him. He opened the first one addressed to Emile

James Jefferson c/o Margaret Jefferson at the old Dagenham address.

Dear Emile
You don't know who I am but I know who you are. I am your sister or half-sister born before you came into this world. Well it appears I am leaving it now as I have a terminal cancer diagnosis. I have instructed my lawyer to leave my estate to you as my only living relative. At least I assume you are still living. It doesn't amount to a fortune but it is a tidy sum.
My love from your sister Vanessa.

Along with the brief letter was the address and telephone number of a lawyer and a clutch of photos of his sister. He looked at the date on the letter and guessed that she had already passed on. It seemed somehow that the women is his life were there for too short a time. No sooner had he found them than they were taken away from him.

xi

While on top of the racing world and in and out of hotels and clubs around the world on the *East Street* campaigns he had to acknowledge he had gotten used to the easy living, to the small luxuries that were a part of that life and though he hated to admit it, he missed it now. Still, he reasoned he could somehow make a living on the island even when shunned by the yachting community.

It took a few months before things settled down and Em got some jobs with an old mate in Southampton who had set up a yacht delivery company a few years previously. Johnno knew Em would be a good bet for some of the deliveries he did to the Mediterranean and across the Atlantic to the Caribbean. It suited Em fine to be sailing again, even if it was to deliver what Johnno called AWB's, 'Average White Boats', for owners who were inexperienced or too time-poor to sail to new cruising grounds themselves.

It was on a delivery trip down to Spain that Em picked up a magazine that had been left on the yacht. *Wooden Boat* magazine, not one he was familiar with. He leafed through it and was soon studying the pictures of beautiful wooden yachts, of the building and restoration of some of these yachts, of woodworking techniques, and the adventures of sailors in some of these graceful boats in far-flung places. This was all a world away from the composite racing boats he had known and the plastic production boats he now delivered to the Mediterranean and Caribbean.

When he got back to the island he ordered a pile of books on wooden boatbuilding and subscribed to *Wooden Boat*. It was as if a new world had opened up. He would almost go as far as a religious conversion. He was in awe of the intricate carpentry that went into these beautiful creations in wood that were at once a working inception of form and function. He read all he could on wooden boat building and thumbed through the copies of *Wooden Boat* like an over-eager schoolboy.

It was on a delivery to Greece on night watch that he determined to build himself a wooden boat that he could pour all his disappointments and angst into and emerge with something beautiful, something pure, a solid wholeness that would cleanse his soul. Not that he was sure he had one. He had been in touch with other boatbuilders and had more or less settled on a Lyle Hess design of a Falmouth Quay Punt – as old fashioned as they come and to Em's eyes, an alluring seductress that he couldn't take his eyes off as he gazed at the plans and the photos of hulls that had been built. Em tried to understand where these feelings have come from and then decided he didn't care. It is his Hallelujah moment, his own Hallelujah, his own pivotal moment in his life where he sloughs off the old and starts again.

xii

Once he was back on the island Em got in touch with the lawyer his sister or half-sister had detailed in her letter. The lawyer expressed some displeasure at Em's tardiness about getting in touch with him but said he would send the relevant documents on. When they arrived Em had to re-read the letter quoting his inheritance several times. It came to nearly £20,000. A fortune to Em and enough to get him started on the embryonic plan in his head to start building his own dream classic boat.

He went down to see Mick, his old friend who had a boatyard of sorts on the edge of the Medina. Like Em, Mick was another lost soul that had gravitated to the island. He had worked on superyachts until the regimentation got to him and he scraped together the money to buy the small yard on the Medina. He specialised in the old one-designs like the X-boat and the Darings and carried out refits on some of the old classics based in Cowes. It was the sort of place to build the boat Em had in mind with piles of timber seasoning in a rack and the redolent smell of sawdust on the floor. And Mick had some of the heavy machinery Em would need to build this boat from the ground up.

Em struck a price with Mick to rent a corner in the old shed in the yard and under Mick's tutelage set about purchasing the hand tools he would need: a set of chisels wrapped in a canvas roll, several different hammers, hand saws and a plane. There were some tools he had no idea about at all like the spokeshave and a sliding bevel until Mick instructed him in their uses. He bought power tools, a drill, and an orbital sander, and again turned to Mick to teach him how to use the big band-saw and the electric bench planer on the wood he would use without removing fingers as well. Without Mick he would have been lost and for a while he was overcome by the weight of learning he realised he needed to do.

When they laid the oak keel for the boat Em stood back and tried to imagine the frames and planking rising skeleton-like from the keel. He was beginning to understand that he was no longer making a living from sailing but that he had found a way of living. There was something honest and true about the wood and the sawdust. He realised now he could look at a plank and do a sort of instant calculation on how tight the grain was and where it might fit on a boat. He could see he would have to laminate timbers for knees and deck beams. He could almost taste the wood.

Em still needed to earn a living and kept doing odd deliveries of boats to the Mediterranean and the Caribbean. He was earning good money, spending little, but the cost of building the boat was greater than he had imagined. To be away from his boat in the shed, his wooden masterpiece, was a wrench. As he delivered boats hither and thither his mind and heart were elsewhere in Mick's yard and the only thing that kept him sane was the knowledge he was tucking money away for the boat.

xiii

It had taken him longer than he envisaged to finish the boat. Mick needed space in the shed and it was going to be a race to launch her before he ran out of money. Now he was nearly there and he would need to agree a time with the long-suffering Mick to launch her.

He had mulled over numerous names for the boat and finally come up with *Selene*, the goddess of the moon, of change, of light, and of sleep. He liked the 'change' part best. He coughed again and wondered if he should book in at the hospital in Newport to see the doctor there. He had missed three appointments already and now *Selene* was ready to launch. Just a few jobs to tidy her up and that rigging needed checking again. In any case, he had an idea of what the diagnosis might be. He had been losing weight and his coughing was getting worse.

Once he had launched her Em told Mick he was going for sea trials. He would be a few days and then back at the yard. Em fired up the engine, slipped the mooring lines and headed out of the Medina River for the Solent. He raised the gaff mainsail and hanked on the working jib. *Selene* heeled slightly and slipped through the water towards the Needles and the western Solent. She sailed like a witch.

Mick hadn't heard from Em for a week when he decided to have a look around the island and see if he could find him. It had been a long week since Em left and he missed his old friend. He kept talking to the empty chair outside the boatshed where Em used to sit. He tracked *Selene* down to Newtown Creek. There was no mistaking the old-fashioned hull of the boat amongst all the AWB's anchored in the creek. He borrowed a dinghy from the small yard at the head of the creek and rowed out to her. There was no answer when he knocked on the hull so he climbed on board to find Em. The main hatch was open and it took just a minute to determine there was no one on board. There was a note on the chart table.

Mick. I knew you would find her. She's yours. This was the best thing I ever did with my life creating this little masterpiece. More than all the silverware, more than all the places I've sailed to, more than life itself. I've given her a bit of a shakedown cruise and everything seems to work as it should. Now she is your girl. Look after her. Em.

Mick took *Selene* back to Cowes and pondered what might have happened. No body was found and the police noted it as a missing person report and possible death by misadventure. Somehow Mick wasn't sure. Would Em do that? All those delivery voyages and nary an accident. He kept seeing the tow-headed Em walking down the street but it was never him. Somehow Mick suspected that one day Em would wander into the yard and join him for a beer. For now, he would make sure he took good care of *Selene*. He ran his hand over the topsides. The gentle curve of the hull seemed to talk to him and he was sure he could hear Em's voice echoing in the ebb tide and the slap of water on the hull.

**FREDDY'S STORY
SHAPED BY LIFE**

i

Freddy adopted his usual position square in front of the counter. Old Ahmed leans over asking him if he is alright, what has he been doing lately, what's that menace of a brother of yours been up to? He says brother like bother. I'm the brother hovering near the rack of spirits in the alcohol section. Freddy looks over to me and I nod. He starts fitting, making awful grunting noises and dribbling while his arms shake uncontrollably. At least that's what Ahmed thinks as he asks Freddy if he is alright. Can he get him something? A glass of water maybe. By this time, I've got the bottle of Bacardi in my parka pocket and I run back over to Freddy.

'Don't worry Mr Ahmed. I'll take him outside. It's normal. He will be OK.' And I wheel Freddy outside and lean over the chair so he can slip the bottle out of my pocket into the inside pocket on the arm of the wheelchair. It's our old routine but we do need to be careful. Some of the shop owners are getting wise to us.

I go back into the shop and apologise to Mr Ahmed. I buy a packet of cigarettes and two cans of lager by way of an impromptu apology and tell Mr Ahmed Freddy is OK now. 'It happens' I say hunching my shoulders. 'But don't worry Mr Ahmed, I'll look after him.'

I push Freddy down the road a bit towards the river. There is a bit of a slope but I'm not doing my normal standing on the two legs at the back and leaning right over Freddy so the chair sits on the ground and gravity takes over. I normally would but sometimes we hit a pothole and the chair goes tits up and Freddy crashes out. Best not to with the bottle of Bacardi on board.

'I thought we were going to the library,' Freddy says. 'I've run out of books. The returns are in with the Bacardi.'

'I thought we could have a beer down by the river,' I reply. 'Then we can go to the library if you want.' Freddy is the reader. I read too, but Freddy devours them. Don't get me wrong – I'm not a dim-wit and have a decent memory for most things. But Freddy is the brains of the outfit – a sort of savant I read somewhere. His specialist subjects are fossils and birds. I can hear him say 'Not that sort of bird'.

My thing is chemistry and cooking. I've been reading lately of how chemistry affects our taste buds and how I can alter the taste of a meal depending on what I use to spice it up. Peanut butter is my favourite at the moment. Freddy reckons my cooking needs to get a whole lot better before I open the chemistry book again. He's talking bollocks because I notice he always wolfs down what I cook for him.

It is not all plain wheeling. We come across Rex and his gang before we get there. At school they think it fun to tip Freddy out of his chair, to rag him as the 'crip with no brains', to tell him 'he shouldn't be at school', that 'he makes the place smell bad.' If it is just Rex, I can take him, but there are too many of his mates with him today. We both keep mum and I steer him through the gang looking straight ahead towards the river. We get to the river and I breathe a sigh of relief and Freddy puts the brakes on next to the bench on the bank. We crack open the beer I have bought and relax by the water. At least the sun is out now.

I'm the older one. Ted. Freddy is my younger brother by two years. He wasn't always in a wheelchair but as his muscles got weaker, he had difficulty walking and so they gave him a wheelchair. Not an electric one but just a bog standard wheelchair. They say he might get an electric chair later if there are funds for it. Are there ever funds? In a way the wheelchair was a relief so I don't have to fit his metal brace and built up shoe – it always took ages in the morning. Now I just bundle him out of bed and get him dressed and into the chair. Easy-Peasy.

ii

I'm the one who looks after him. Our mum works cleaning jobs, whatever she can get, and is dog-tired when she gets in of an evening. I'm getting to be quite a good cook although Freddy reckons my curry is pants compared to the Indian in town. How would he know? How would I know? We have only ever been to the Indian once nor to any other restaurant for that matter. I don't think fast food counts. As long as mum gets a glass of brandy in her hand, she is fine with whatever I am cooking, though she has started to get weepy of late and tells us that this life was not what she intended for us. Actually, I'm fine with it and am thinking about training as a chef.

I won't say we are like blood brothers. We are more normal than that and bicker and argue over all sorts of shit. But against the world we are together which is pretty inevitable given our intimacy. I mean I bath Freddy, get him on and off the toilet though thank god he can wipe his own bum, undress him and put his pyjamas on ready for bed and dress him again in the morning. It's all pretty normal for us now.

But it's the other stuff that worries me. At night I need to stay awake for a while to make sure the demons don't emerge from the whorls on the green wallpaper in our room. I'm not sure exactly what they are or where they come from. I watch the wall intently and though I don't know where they come from, I do know they mean us no good. And I watch when mum goes out to a car with one our 'uncles' in it. I mean they park right under a streetlamp and the whole bloody neighbourhood can see what's happening. Freddy always asks me what's going on and where has mum gone and I just tell him she is out talking to someone. He knows I'm lying.

Just lately one of the 'uncles' has been visiting more often and mum often invites him into the house. Ozzy is a fat bastard who smells of beer and fags. Mum introduces him and Freddy and I say hullo and then hightail it out the backdoor. Our little council house backs on to Parkhurst Forest and we can get the wheelchair through the gate at the back and in a few minutes, we are in the woods. Have to say that wheelchair takes the rough stuff OK when I balance it on its back wheels and we can get down the path without Freddy tumbling out. Not that he minds too much, well not at first unless he thinks I'm doing it intentionally.

iii

I know mum has always had it hard on her own but I'm here and I'm the one looking after Freddy. In the forest we can wheel our way out to the carpark and then down into town. You might ask what we do with the booze we have been nicking from the corner shops and you might just be surprised. Freddy wants a new camera and has set his heart on a Canon something or other. I only know it's expensive. As usual he has read all the reviews and so we have been saving for this bloody expensive camera. We take the booze down to Jim's pub in town and in the carpark do a transaction – usually around half what it costs in the shop. Usually we get £10 for a bottle of Bacardi after a bit of haggling with Jim. So far, we have around half the cost of the camera saved up.

This time, what with Ozzy around, we hang about in the forest for a bit. Sometimes we offer to clean the windscreens of the cars in the forest carpark which works out OK because I think they take pity on Freddy holding the bucket of soapy water in the wheelchair while I squeegee the windscreen. We are an odd combo. Everyone around here says 'hullo' to me in a normal voice and then leans close to Freddy to ask him in a slow monotone.

'Hel-lo … young-man… How… are… you?' Then they look at me for an answer as if Freddy can't understand them.

'I'm… fine… tha-nk… you' Freddy replies.

We usually get talking with them for a bit. They are well-meaning people but because Freddy is in a wheelchair, they assume he is mentally incapacitated. After a bit Freddy gets bored with the game and I will knock my knee into the back of the chair and Freddy will do his fitting act. I will explain he is getting tired and we need to get off. We have a bit of a laugh about it between ourselves and continue on our way.

Mind you in the last couple of days there has been a creepy man hanging around watching us from the bench on the edge of the park. I haven't seen him around before and worry a bit about him. He doesn't talk to us but just watches us though he avoids any direct gaze. It's OK when there are lots of dog-walkers around, but now the carpark is empty and he's there and I'm feeling a bit spooked.

I'm not sure why he rattles me – he's dressed quite smartly but the stubble and hair don't fit somehow. There is something, just something about him. I worry even more when we start to trundle across the carpark to the main road and he gets up from the bench and walks over to us.
'Hello Ted. Hello Freddy' he says looking at me.
'Don't worry boys I just want a word.'

For a minute I get really worried. Maybe he is some sort of undercover cop who is going to arrest us for nicking booze in the corner shops. But he doesn't look right for that. Or some sort of pervert. A serial killer?

He talks in a raspy breathy voice. 'I'm not sure how to say this. You don't know me and I don't really know you. Except I sort of know who you are. I'm your father and I know you won't remember me but I was around at the beginning.' He smiles, a crooked forced sort of smile. I'm not sure what to say as mum has always told us to say our father is dead if anyone asks.

'How do we know you are who you say you are?' Freddy asks. I nod in agreement with Freddy – why didn't I think of that? 'You could be anyone', Freddy continues, 'Since we have no idea who our father was or anything about him. We were too little when he left so he may as well be dead.'

The man looks a bit dejected at this. 'Listen', he says, 'I know it was a long time ago, but life isn't always simple. My name, if you are interested, is Jack. Jack Bilkman. Your mother took her maiden name when I left and changed yours too and I don't blame her. But I want to make amends in a way. Listen, do you two want a drink in the pub? I know you are a bit young Freddy but we can sit outside. You know. You can have something fizzy and maybe a sausage roll or something else?'

Freddy pulls a face and looks doubtful. What if this guy is some sort of pervert who figures a boy in a wheelchair is easy pickings? Then again, they can go to Jim's pub where he knows them. That would be safe.

I look at Freddy who nods. 'Yeah. OK. The Green I say.'

Jack nods. 'Yeah. That would be OK. Shall I push Freddy?'

I mouth 'NO' and steer him towards town and the river. Jack, our father or so he says, walks in front of us so at least I feel more secure that way. Freddy turns around to me and raises an eyebrow quizzically. I shake my head to indicate I have no idea what is going on. Here we are trundling down to town with a complete stranger who professes to be our father returned from god knows where. I guess it was this or back to the house with mum and 'uncle' Ozzy. Not a lot in it really.

iv

The Green sits on the edge of the River Medina looking across to the yachts and hulks and a few houseboats tied up off the Odessa yard. It's a local pub and Jim the landlord actively discourages any stray tourists from drinking there. We go to the outside tables by the carpark where we are on our own and Jim comes out to greet us. I can see he is a little put out that Jack is there though he does appear to know him.

'Hello George' Jim says, 'What can I get you? I know what the boys want.' I look at Freddy and mouth 'George?' I look at Jack or George and shake my head.

After Jim has gone back inside Jack drops his head and looks away. 'I know this sounds strange but I use a different name here in town.' He seems weary and almost tearful. 'Listen boys. I want to give you something to make amends for the things I've done wrong. This is from your father.' He leans over to Freddy and hands him a thick padded envelope. 'Hide that in your chair' he says. 'Hide it good when you get home. It's my contribution to make amends for all the time I was away. I made a bit of money in Australia and so this is your share. Don't look now and keep it safe for yourselves.' Freddy is tempted then tucks it into the inside pocket on the chair without looking inside the envelope.

Jim returns with three beers. When he leaves Jack gets up and looks around him. He is agitated by something and shakes his head and then abruptly says goodbye to us without even taking a sip of his beer. 'Sorry lads. Can't explain but I'd get going as well if I was you two', he says over his shoulder to us as he walks off down the path along the river. I watch him and notice he is still looking around him as if he is about to be pursued. His body seems to sag as if with a weight, the weight of the world don't they say, on his shoulders. I take a deep gulp of my beer and motion to Freddy it's time to go and we start the trek back home. It's all bloody uphill.

On the bridge across the Medina we stop to look down on the river like we always do. The murky water of the Medina flows sluggishly out to sea. It must be low water I reckon as the boats alongside are all sitting on the mud. I look out to where Jack or whatever his name really is walks towards the old light industrial unit by the river. For a moment he turns around and for some reason I duck below the bridge barrier though it is unlikely he will spot us on the bridge. I'm more relieved than fearful now he has gone.

We hear the police sirens before we see the cars. Several police cars are driving at speed down the river path before screeching to a halt. Policeman and some plain clothes cops are running towards a figure that must be Jack. Everyone is out of the pub now watching the action going on by the riverbank. From the bridge we see him forced to lie flat on the concrete and his hands cuffed behind his back. I look at Freddy and decide we really need to hightail it out of here. So far no-one seems to be looking for us.

iv

When we get back to the house Mum and Ozzy are busy drinking and canoodling in the living room so we go to our bedroom. Freddy looks in the envelope and lets out a whistle and a long slow 'shit'. I put my finger to my lips to hush him lest Mum hears us. Freddy shows me the envelope. It is packed full of banknotes. I mean really packed with fifties and twenties and everything.

'There's more than enough for a camera in here', Freddy says. 'Jesus, there's enough for a new wheelchair and to send you to college for that bloody chef's course. And then some left over.' I take a look and sure enough there is more money in the envelope than I've ever seen in my life.

'We need to hide this' I say to Freddy. 'I'll put it in your fossil collecting bag in the wardrobe.' Freddy nods and we sit there, dumbfounded and wondering where the money came from. And who the hell is Jack? Or George? Is he really our father and if he is will the police come around to question us? I've a feeling I'm going to be checking the news on the radio all night.

It's not long before Island Radio reports the police raid on the river. His name is George Millar and he had recently been released from Parkhurst along with his cell-mate Jack Bilkman. Together they had retrieved the proceeds of an armed robbery Jack Bilkman had carried out before going to jail. Freddy and I are at a loss. The radio news-reader says George Millar has been arrested for the murder of Jack Bilkman two days ago. No trace of the money has yet been found. I look at Freddy and put a finger to my lips again. 'No one needs to know. No one.'

V

I am angry at them all. At my mother. My 'uncles'. At everyone. When Freddy died they all came to the funeral, stood around talking amongst themselves, argued a bit, then went to the pub for a wake. They went to the wrong pub. If they had gone to the Green where Freddy was known that would have been better, but no, they went to the Waterside. That was their pub.

The only one who seemed sad about Freddy's death was Mr Ahmed from the corner shop. I don't know how he found out about the funeral but there he was. He looked over to me and shook his head, a sad smile on his face. I knew then that he had known about us nicking stuff from his shop though he had never said anything. Had never called the cops.

Freddy got a bad bout of pneumonia after we had been mucking around the car park and the forest and it started to rain. Usually I had an old raincoat with me that I tucked around him in the chair but for some reason I'd forgotten it.

Freddy's muscles had got weaker and he wheezed when he breathed, taking big gulps of air down to his compressed lungs. He took to his bed and that night when he started vomiting some awful white spew I went into see mother about what we should do. She was a few brandies down by that stage and told me to wait for the morning to see if he was better. I called an ambulance.

The paramedic didn't take long to decide Freddy needed to go to hospital - pronto. I packed a few things for Freddy and rode along in the back of the ambulance as it made the short trip down to St Mary's Hospital. They wheeled him in and a nice nurse showed me to a chair and asked if I wanted a cup of tea. Tea! I needed a glass of Mum's brandy but I didn't say that and thanked her and asked when I might go into the ward and see Freddy. She said she would tell me when they had run some tests and got him comfortable. I was nearly in tears with everyone fussing over him and looking out for him. Of course, I bloody didn't cry.

vi

I stayed in the hospital that night. The nice nurse suggested I get something to eat in the canteen because it was closing soon and then brought me a blanket and said I could sleep on the chairs in the waiting room.

'You're a good boy' she says. 'I phoned your mother and she said she will be here tomorrow. Do you usually look after your brother?'

I nodded. 'She is probably busy' I say. Probably busy having a drink and messing with Ozzy. She doesn't come in the morning or the afternoon. Another nurse was in and out, a pretty dark haired woman who fussed over me just as the other one had. I could live here. Mum arrives that evening and sits next to me. 'What's happening Ted? Is Freddy OK? I don't know what to do, who to turn to. Why does this always happen to me?' She smells of booze and when she starts crying I don't know what to do. If she was really worried why hadn't she come down with Freddy last night?

'I suppose if you are here there is no point me being here' she says. 'I may as well go home. They will ring me if anything happens.' I nod again and she gets up and leaves. Just like that. She hasn't even asked if she can see Freddy.

The first nurse is on her shift again. In the early evening she comes and sits next to me. She looks at me and I can tell the news isn't good. 'Ted' she says. 'Ted… I don't think Freddy is going to last through the night. Why don't you come in with me and sit by his bed?' I sit there though the evening holding his hand. It is cold and clammy. I talk to him about anything I can think of. Cameras. Wheelchairs. Electric wheelchairs. I tell him we have the money now and we can get all that stuff. Every now and then his eyes flutter and he looks at me and I know he is trying to smile.

And then the machine above him starts to beep continuously. The nurse comes in and then another nurse. Then a man in blue scrubs who I find out is the doctor. They look at the machines beeping above him, at one another, then at me.

The machines wail on, the noise of despair and death. I know that. They usher me out and the nice nurse gets me a cup of tea and sits me down. 'I've phoned your mother' she whispers. 'She said she will be down some time.'

vii

I was angry at them all at the funeral. I still am. It's probably why I went off the rails a bit and started to act a bit strange. I left school and bunked off down by the river. I would sit down there and one of the guys living on an old sailing boat took me under his wing. I hadn't tried any of the stuff Rex and his gang probably used. Weed. Coke. Poppers. Uppers and downers. But Charlie on the boat got me into it. Well into weed and coke. The inside of Charlie's boat smelt of weed all the time and every so often he would pull out a small mirror and do lines of coke. I sort of went along with it.

I don't blame Charlie. I blame all the others who didn't give a toss about Freddy. For my keep at

Charlies I used to deliver some of his drugs to various pubs. Just weed and some coke. Pushing a wheelchair around had given me strong hands and shoulders and with a gut full of anger nobody wanted to bother me. I was just under six foot by now and quick on my feet.

It happened with Rex and his lot. They were hanging around the Green where I was delivering some of Charlie's little bags of coke for some regulars. Rex called me out.

'Look. It's the crip's brother. What are you doing here Teddy boy?'

I ignore him. I've got things to do so I walk past looking for my regulars I need to deliver to. Rex won't leave it alone.

'Come on you little wanker. Bit lost without your brother are you?' He grabs me by the shoulder. 'You shouldn't be here. You smell bad.'

People like Rex have no idea of what they are walking into. He is as thick as shit. Thicker. I snap and swing around to face him. I'm not worried for myself and for a second I see a flicker of hesitation on Rex's face. I go straight for his throat and tighten my hand around his neck, flip him over onto the ground and keep squeezing his windpipe. He starts to turn grey and I can hear shouts around me and hands trying to pull me off Rex. I hold on and squeeze his neck like I'm holding onto Freddy's wheelchair and pushing uphill for my life.

viii

Someone must have called the rozzers and they arrived as some of the regulars were pulling me off Rex. I was snarling and lashing out like a madman, all the anger at Freddy's death spilling out of me. One of the bobbys put handcuffs on me and then looked me in the eye and told me to calm down or he would put me in the police wagon and let me cool down there. Funny. His gaze and demeanour somehow made me stop and realise I was in deep shit. I still had Charlie's bags of dope in my coat pocket.

When they searched me it didn't take them long to find the bags.

'What's this?' the bobby asks. I shrugged my shoulders. He looked concerned and nodded towards the police car. 'Best we go down the station.'

The bobby sat me down and asked if I wanted a lawyer or someone to accompany me while I was being questioned. I didn't.

'My name is Mark' he said, 'And I have to tell you that you are in deep do-do here. I've checked the records and you don't appear to have any previous convictions. I rang your mother and she will come down to the station tomorrow. What I can say is that you can get up to five years for supplying this amount of Class A and B drugs. As you have no previous convictions that will likely be less as long as you help us out with our enquiries.'

The bobby had a slight accent though his English was probably better than mine. I told him I didn't know who supplied the stash. I just picked it up from a rubbish bin down on the quay. He didn't buy it.

Soon another plain clothes copper came in and sat down listening to Mark. After ten minutes he held up his hand to Mark. 'Throw the book at him. I've got a pretty good idea who the main dealer is and he will spill his guts and blame this little shit for everything. They always do. So just book him.'

Mark looked at me kindly after the plain clothes copper had gone. 'Listen Ted. Unless you are looking forward to prison I need some mitigating circumstances. Why don't you tell me a bit about yourself?'

I have to say I wasn't sure what mitigating circumstances were or what exactly he wanted. Or if I could trust him. Under the harsh glare of the strip light and after a bit of deep breathing I figure it wouldn't hurt to tell him about Freddy and life at home. Maybe it would give me some leeway in all of this to figure out what to do next. So, I tell him about Freddy and how no-one had really helped us. About life at home. About life here in Newport and Rex and his crew.

'Is that who you were fighting with?' Mark asked. Ted nodded. 'He and his lot used to pick on me and Freddy. If I wasn't around they thought it funny to tip Freddy out of his wheelchair. Used to call him names. You know, like crip or drongo or moron. That sort of thing.' Ted looks at this Mark to see if he was getting any of this and was surprised to see that the policeman looked troubled by what he heard.

'What you are saying is that circumstances beyond your control led you to this life. Did it?' Mark looks at him and nods his head to indicate a yes from Ted. Ted wonders if this Mark believes any of this shit that he is suggesting to him. Surely not. Anyway, he nods his head in agreement. It is dawning on him that he is in deep do-do here and this Mark policeman is trying to lessen the load. Ted nods again. 'If they had only known Freddy was brighter than any of them,' he added.

They kept me in the local clink for two weeks before I came up in front of the magistrate. Mark came every other day to see me and said he was surprised I was not out on bail. 'Probably the Class A drugs you had on you,' he says. Mum came down as well and I was surprised she didn't give me a bollocking. She seemed upset at me being locked up and said she had tried to get me out on bail. I knew she didn't have any money anyway so wasn't too worried. I mean it's warm in here, you get fed every day and they even got me some books to read.

I pleaded guilty at the hearing. There was really no point in denying anything and Mark was there to tell the magistrate I had been helpful in their enquiries and described my life with Freddy. Mum was there as well blubbing away and I suppose that all helped. I was given eighteen months in the Juvenile Detention Centre at Parkhurst though afterwards Mark says to me I will probably only do nine months or maybe less for good behaviour. 'You can do courses there he says, you know business courses and stuff like that. I think you would be good at that. Any clues what you might want to do.' I didn't have any then but as it turned out, they did a Food Hygiene course and I got to train as a chef like I always wanted.

ix

Mark was right. I got out in nine months with a diploma in food hygiene and business management. On his last visit Mark told me I should get a job as a chef in town and make sure I didn't reoffend. 'You go in again and you will be doing time in the main prison block and I can tell you it's nothing like the Juvenile Offenders Unit you have just been in. Trust me.'

I did. I returned home again and retrieved the envelope of money we had secreted in Freddy's fossil bag. Mum wanted to know what she should do with Freddy's stuff. 'Keep it a bit and I'll look after it,' I say to her. 'I'd like to look after his stuff you know.' She nods her head and looks kind of sad. 'What's up?' I ask her. 'Why so sad?' She mumbles something about losing both her boys and for a minute I want to go and hug her and tell her everything will be alright. And then Ozzy comes into the room and looks at me like I'm an unwanted shithole from another life. I suppose I am and I leave mum with just a peck on the cheek.

I decided to leave Newport and live up the road in Cowes. It's a small island but there are different vibes in different parts of it. It was really to get away from my hometown. Even just a few miles up the road. And besides there were plenty of restaurants and cafes in Cowes.

I found a room in Cowes and set about looking for a job. That proved to be pretty easy as the flu outbreak had decimated the numbers who wanted to work in hospitality. My only slight drawback was my police record. My trump card was the food hygiene certificate.

Turns out they were so desperate to get staff in Cowes that I had a choice of where to work. I started as a commis chef in a cafe on the High Street. It served the usual stuff including a full English breakfast and a range of dishes for lunch like burgers, chilli, sausages and egg, that sort of stuff. Shit, we ate better in Parkhurst. Same sort of stuff but better cooked.

After a few months I suggested to the owner that I could make up some real stocks and sauces for the meals instead of opening the freezer or getting a packet down off the shelf. I must have hurt his feelings as I think his words were something like 'Perhaps you should try the kitchen in Parkhurst instead of trying to teach me how to cook. Collect your stuff…'

My sacking had a rainbow at the end. I applied for a job to be commis chef in the restaurant in the up-market Castle Hill Hotel which is one of the poshest restaurants in Cowes. Harry the maître-d' interviewed me and seemed more amused than upset when I related the story about the café and getting the sack from it. He took me into the kitchen and turned me over to Jackson the head chef. 'Get him to whip up a few things Jackson and then we will have a think about him.'

A simple green salad with cherry tomatoes and capers and my own vinaigrette, a Hollandaise sauce that was a bit thin, and some shortcrust pastry, all inspected by Jackson and the other commis chef. A few hours later and Jackson bundled me out to Harry again. 'He'll do,' was all Jackson says to Harry while I was grinning inside. This place was a whole different ballgame to Parkhurst and the café.

X

I worked my butt off in the kitchen learning all the tricks of the trade and how to properly prep for dishes. This was a high-end restaurant with a firm grip on the basics but often with a subtle twist to a dish. Some were bizarre but worked like dark chocolate and peanut butter in a chilli - only the restaurant called it the Chilli Queen.

Often times I caught a glimpse of Freddy sitting in his chair smiling at me and giving me a thumbs up as I beavered away in the kitchen and I knew he would have been proud of me crawling out of the swamp and getting this far. I also get the feeling he was telling me there was more on the horizon.

I worked in the Castle Hill for a year honing my skills and learning what people wanted from a kitchen. At the end of the year Harry calls me in and Jackson is there as well. He offers me the job of rota chef for the restaurant. Apparently Jackson is chuffed with my work in the kitchen. While I'm tempted I have a little germ of an idea myself and I've talked it over with Freddy as you do with a dead brother.

Often the owners and captains of yachts racing in Cowes, and there is a lot of racing that goes on here, will ask the restaurant if they can prepare lunch boxes for the crew when racing out on the water. The restaurant always said 'no'. It wasn't what they did. 'Concentrate on what we do well and leave that sort of stuff for the little people,' was what Harry said with what I thought was a pretty patronising tone. For some reason Freddy put it in my head that I should take our money and set up a business supplying the red trouser and blazer brigade with lunch boxes.

I don't think Harry at the Castle Hill believed me when I said I was setting up on my own. He offered me more money but I explained to him it was not the money, not the restaurant or the people, I had learnt so much here and I was sad to leave. It was just something I had to do. Me and Freddy.

xi

One other thing Parkhurst did for me was put me on that business management course so I knew I had to plan this all out carefully. In my spare time I tried out a number of places that were doing lunch and snack boxes for the racing yachts. There was only one place that did any decent grub and that was still limited to a few quiches and filled rolls – good stuff but limited. I also

noted that the presentation of the food was rubbish, often in flimsy carboard or
aluminium foil cartons like you get from Indian restaurants. I wanted different. And finding somewhere to base it all was not going to be easy.

I had about £3000 from mine and Freddy's stash, from 'our father', and that would have to do. The banks wouldn't even look at loaning me money what with a criminal record. I found an old kebab shop on Mill Hill Road that had a basic kitchen and a shop front for a good lease price. It needed a bit of work but I reckoned I could set it up for my takeaway food. I even had a name: Freddy's Posh Nosh.

It took a little while for me to knock the old kebab shop into shape and a bit longer before I realised I couldn't do this on my own. I advertised in the local rag for someone to help with the prepping of the food and delivering it to the boats as well. Most of those that turned up were wasters. The one surprise was Susie Amato. She was a tall willowy type with long black hair and heavy black glasses and a diamond piercing in her nose. At first the diamond put me off but I was wrong. She had cycled over for the interview from Wootton Bridge and I pretty much knew after starting to interview her that she would get the job. It also put the germ of an idea in my head: we would get a tricycle with a tray on the back to deliver the lunch packs to the boats.

Susie was a revelation. Her parents were Italian and had settled here after the war. Her given name was Susanna but she always went by Susie. She was the youngest in the family, a 'mistake' she told me later, and when her mother died she had looked after her father, nursed him and cooked for him until he too died. She had ideas about the menu we should have and together we tried out all sorts of combinations. We came up with the following list first:
Mini-quiches normal Lorraine and tomato, basil and parmesan
Baguette with chicken and lettuce or chicken, lime and mint with rocket
BLT on sourdough
Frittata with salmon and zucchini
Salmon and potato salad

Tuna pasta salad with anchovies and sun dried tomatoes
Cheese and tomato toasties
Pizza with tomato and peperoni or straight Margherita

Anyone at the Castle Hill Hotel would have recognised a few of the recipes though I'm sure they didn't mind. It was an ambitious start but Susie and I cooked them all and tried them cold. Then we looked at how to pack them. And how to price them. I figured that the lunchboxes could have a selection of items for a set price so they needed to be ordered in advance. Then we would have assorted selection boxes for the forgetful ones who just wanted to grab a lunchbox in the morning.

Things were slow at first but soon word of mouth upped the orders and by the end of the year I needed more help in the kitchen. Then it hit me. I went back up to the Juvenile Detention Centre at Parkhurst and asked the instructor if he had any candidates that were shaping up well and would be released soon… or early if they had a job. He looked amused. 'Have a word with Jezza. The fat one over there. He's pretty good though maybe not as fast as you were to pick the trade up.' He calls Jezza over and I proposition him. 'Hard work. Bugger all social life. Possibility of advancement if you are good enough.' Jezza looked puzzled. 'You really want to employ me?' I nod. 'You bet.'

We all work long hours. Jezza would finish up earlier and head back to Newport where he lived with his mum. Susie and I work on a bit later, sometimes a lot later, and would finish up having a glass or two of wine afterwards. Somehow, she still manages to cycle off back home to her little flat in Wootton. I sleep out the back in the storeroom on a little single bed with all the cardboard cartons and packs of napkins and an old fridge-freezer wheezing away with some of our prepped food in it.

I suppose it was inevitable that Susie and I would team up. Bit of a surprise since I am a twenty year old virgin. I have no idea about Susie but one night she steered me into the storeroom and kissed me tenderly on the neck. Next thing I know we are both in the little rickety bed and I get my first introduction to the art of tender lovemaking. Miraculously it all works and we become an item with lots of hard work and late night tenderness. I have never been so happy or, for that matter, so exhausted. Jezza has worked out fine but the business is booming and we need a new kitchen and another trainee from Parkhurst.

One of the stranger outcomes of all this is that everyone calls me Freddy. I guess they assume from the name 'Freddy's Posh Nosh' that I am Freddy. At first I correct them and then I give up. I am Freddy. Even Susie calls me Freddy though I've yet to explain to her why it's 'Freddy's Posh Nosh' and I'm Teddy.

After a bit of looking around I found a restaurant down on Medina Road that had gone bust. I made an offer and the owner nearly bit my hand off. Seems the last tenant hadn't been up to date with his payments. Susie and I got a team in and we soon had the kitchen sorted and could carry on while closing down the Mill Hill kitchen. It was about this time that Susie, ever the mover and shaker, suggested we get a flat together nearby. She had sold her place for a good price and I had some spare cash even after leasing the old restaurant on Medina Road. We bought a little two-up-two-down in nearby York Street and settled in – well as much as we could with the business booming.

xii

What happened with 'Freddy's Posh Nosh' is that we were not only doing sailing lunch boxes but picnic boxes for land-based groups as well. Not too many but it fills up the gaps between regattas and such in Cowes. By now there were five of us working in the kitchen and delivering nosh to boats and groups. I used to wander down to the marinas at times and by now I knew a lot of the skippers on the racing yachts there. That's how I met Em and Sophie.

It was Sophie who latched onto me as one of her little projects. Em was not around a lot of the time and whenever I was down in the marina promoting Freddy's Posh Nosh and getting orders she would beckon me on board and then buttonhole other skippers as they walked along the pontoon and extoll the virtues of my 'posh nosh'. She was popular around the marina and I couldn't have pulled in the punters like she did. She had a loud infectious laugh and would rib the other skippers and crew mercilessly until they signed up for my lunchboxes. For me it was more than just the orders. I felt a bit like I was Sophie's brother who needed to look out for her if needs be. Not that she needed much looking after. She was feisty as heck. But you know what I mean.

I'm sure lots of the crew down there wondered what was going on with Sophie being so familiar with me. I knew lots of them regarded me as a bit of an oik and I suppose in a way I was. The main trimmer on *East Street* was a tall lad called Sebastian. Wavy blonde hair, knobby public school accent, always a little put down to me and at times to Sophie as well. He resented the fact that she was boat captain and often intimated that he should be. I would hear him talking to Em and trying to persuade him that he should be given Sophie's job. I also noticed he took Bridgewater aside a few times in an animated conversation I guessed was along the same lines. Fat chance there when Em lived with Bridgewater's daughter.

I guess it was inevitable that the whole affair would blow up. Sebastian and Sophie had been having a war of words for a while and eventually it erupted into a mega-argument between them. I was sitting on board with Sophie when Sebastian stormed out of the cabin with his bags and started ripping into Sophie. She was not one to mess with and soon ordered him off the boat and told him not to come back.

Sebastian threw his bags onto the pontoon and then started in. 'Listen you little rich bitch. You may think you have seen the last of me but not so. And as for your common little moron from the island, well you can fuck him all you want but daddy will hear about it.' Before Sophie could stop me I was up on the pontoon. Sebastian might have been taller than me but he didn't reckon with mixing it with a boy who had grown up rough in Newport. 'Come on you little oik. I'll break all your teeth before you blink.' He swung at me and I moved just enough for him to hit my shoulder and be off balance. Then I grabbed him by the neck and brought my knee up into his balls. I pushed him backwards and he flopped onto the pontoon with a thud. He must have hit his head because he gave a sort of moan and then went limp.

By this time some of the others on the pontoon were running up to grab me so I put up my hands and backed off. Sebastian got to his feet and shook his head. Sophie was screaming at them that Sebastian had started it all and to leave me alone. Not that they looked that keen after seeing Sebastian prone on the pontoon. With others around from boat crews on the pontoon Sebastian regained some of his confidence and old arrogance though I noticed he kept his distance from me. For a moment I thought he wanted to have another go at me but instead he lashed out at Sophie. 'Not the last you have heard of this you common bitch. I'll get you back for this don't you worry about that. I'll see you done.' Before I went for him again he was ushered up the pontoon.

It didn't take long for Em to arrive on the scene. Either someone told him or he was on his way here anyway. He nodded towards me and then hopped on *East Street* with a face like thunder. I heard him start up at Sophie asking, 'What the fuck was happening?' before saying 'This sort of shit is no way to run a boat. What the hell happened with Sebastian?' I decided I was well out of it and marched up the pontoon to go to the shop. It hadn't been a good day and my shoulder was starting to throb where Sebastian had hit it.

Things cooled down a bit after that and the next day when I was down in the marina getting orders Sophie beckoned me on board. 'You OK?' she asked. 'Don't worry as that Sebastian won't be back. Only problem is that his father is a big cheese at the Squadron and will probably make problems for my dad. Em is a bit pissed off, make that really pissed off that this whole thing kicked off and wants me to keep you at a distance. I'm not really sure we should be seen together that much. Sorry Freddy... it's just... life.' She looked a bit sad on telling me this but I wasn't entirely surprised. I agreed though I have to say I was a bit pissed off as well. I had only been protecting her and now it seemed I was being scrubbed out.

I got angry as I walked up the hill back to the kitchen. This casual brush-off had shades of my life with Freddy about it, shades of being looked down on, of being little worth to anyone, of what others thought was my rightful place on the bottom of the ladder. I was sinking into some dark place just like when Freddy died.

xiii

I heard about Sophie the day after it happened. The rumour mill was going big time in town with all sorts of accounts of what had happened. And how. And why. I wasn't that surprised when a couple of policemen turned up at the kitchen and asked to have a word with me. Just routine they said.

I told them what they wanted to know which wasn't much. Had I been down at the marina that day? Had I talked to Sophie recently? Did I know anyone who had a grudge against her? I answered their questions as best I could. But not quite.

I had been down in the marina that day. Just on the dock not on the pontoons. I used to go down and sit there some evenings after work. When the storm brewed up I went down partly out of curiosity and partly in case I was needed to help with any of the yachts there. Well, *East Street* in particular. I don't know exactly why I was there and I saw very little.

But I couldn't tell those policemen that given my criminal record. You see something like that haunts you forever even though you might have changed things and turned your life around. But those guys never believe you. A leopard can never change its spots as my mum used to say. I don't think that's true.

MARK'S STORY
SHAPED BY LOSS

i

Mark looked at the letter again and wondered what to do. He had retired from the force two years ago to look after his wife in what proved to be the final year of her life. And now they wanted him to come back and take charge of an old case he had worked on years ago – god, how many years ago had that been? The letter was from the Assistant Chief Constable in Southampton and so, Mark surmised, of some import. He knew police numbers on the island had been below the normal levels but still he was surprised they wanted to re-open the old case he had worked on some four or five years ago. Still his coffers were low and his early retirement to look after Mary had depleted his pension.

He thought back to all those years ago, it must be forty years or more, when he had walked off the fishing boat he was employed on and had sought asylum in Hull. The government minder on board who was supposed to keep an eye on them was an alcoholic who necked at least a bottle of vodka a day and when the crew went for their run ashore he had been asleep in an alcoholic haze. It had all been so easy.

ii

Mark Krajewski had arrived on the island by a long and twisting route. Born in Poland he had signed onto a trawler when he was twenty-two and was soon on a boat trawling in the Baltic and the North Sea. He had long nurtured a desire to escape to the west and on one of the trawlers forays into the North Sea he decided to try his luck at escaping communist Poland when the boat docked at Hull to unload its catch.

He was surprised at how easy it was. The crew were given leave for a run ashore in the evening and armed with an address in Hull that offered assistance to Poles escaping to the United

Kingdom, he wandered off from the group, knocked on the door of the address he had been given and was ushered inside. Here he was greeted by a Polish woman, Malgorzata, though she now used the English equivalent of Margaret she informed Mark, who gave him some paperwork to fill in and a cup of tea.

'Tomorrow you will go to the British Embassy with these documents and inform them you want to defect from Poland because you have been, let's say, treated badly there and your life is in danger.' She laughed. 'It might be now you have deserted your boat without official permission – but probably not. Just joking.'

In the morning Mark took the papers he had filled into the embassy and within an hour had a document to say he had applied for asylum and his case would be reviewed in the coming months. He registered down at the police station and then went for a coffee. As he sat in the café he couldn't help but reflect on the difference between Hull and Gdansk in his native Poland where he had been just a few short months ago.

Here the officials had treated him with some disdain but with a politeness that officials in Gdansk had never had, at least in his experience.
Everyone knew they held the power to do whatever they liked and they made it plain to you they had that power. Here he was free to go. He went back to the house where they had already arranged for him to be accommodated in another Polish household in Hull and suggested he get some work, maybe 'on the black.'

Mark worked on building sites around the city. He would turn up at the docks in Hedon Street with other casual labourers and gang bosses would stop by to pick up labour for a job somewhere in the city. They were always paid in cash at the end of the day and Mark quite liked the casual nature of it all. On weekends he went to the public library where he joined a class teaching English to foreigners. Soon his English was good enough for him to sit an exam to get a diploma in the language. He had always been a quick learner. After a year in Hull he was granted full residency and he decided it was time to look for a more permanent job.

iii

It was around this time that he came face to face with the seamier side to Hull. Walking back from the library one night a man jumped out of an alleyway and thrust a knife in his face.

'Give me your money shitface or I'll put this in you.' He wiggled the knife in Mark's face. Mark hesitated only a second or two before he knocked the man's hand away and punched him on the nose. The man squealed and backed off for a minute before whistling a long low note. Suddenly Mark found himself surrounded by three more men with knives.

Mark nodded. 'OK. Here's the money', he said pulling his wallet out. It had over two hundred pounds in it and he was reluctant to let it go. The first man who had attacked him grabbed the wallet and looked inside. 'Not such a hero now are you shitface?' He nodded to the others and picked up his knife. In a flash he stuck it in Mark's shoulder. 'That's for my nose shitface. Next time just give me your money.'

The group disappeared into the alley as Mark slumped to the ground. His shoulder was pumping blood out and he wondered if the knife had severed some critical artery. A short while later he was found and someone raised the alarm and called an ambulance and the police.

He woke up in hospital with his shoulder bandaged up and an IV line in his arm. At least, he thought, I'm alive and here. The doctor later told him he had been lucky. The knife narrowly missed his axillary artery in the shoulder and he could have bled to death from the knife wound. 'You were lucky', he said and tapped the hospital notes on the bed. 'Don't do it again', he said with a smile.

The next day a policeman arrived to take the particulars of the mugging and to ask him to report to the police station for a formal interview when he was released from the hospital. 'Nothing to worry about', the policeman intoned as he left. 'Just tidying up loose ends.'

The few days Mark spent in the hospital changed the way he looked at things. Everyone here had been kind to him, friendly even, getting him to hospital and calming him down. Even the policeman had been so patient instructing him to take it easy and get down to the station when he could.

The nurses had mollycoddled him bringing him tea and coffee and then letting him out so he could sit out on the verandah with a cigarette. This was more than he had known growing up in Poland and he decided there and then that he would do something useful for the people of this new country he now lived in. Something unfolded inside him and he looked around him with new eyes. He just didn't know what he would do yet.

iv

When he was released from hospital, he went down to the police station as requested. His father had been a policeman in Gdansk until the first demonstrations when he had resigned and then been arrested for helping the demonstrations. Mark had been only dimly aware of any of this and when his father disappeared – 'Don't talk about it to anyone boy' his mother had sternly told him – he tucked it all behind him and made sure he kept clear of the police.

Now here he was sitting in an office with a cup of tea giving his account of what happened, of what he remembered, to the young constable who had visited him in hospital. He seemed so young and Mark couldn't help asking why he had joined the police.

The young constable smiled at him and gave a rambling explanation of growing up on an estate in Hull, dodging the gangs that roamed the estate, and then with a sad smile said 'And then they killed my older brother. The particulars are not important and at first I just wanted to avenge his murder. Then I thought the better plan was to take them on as a policeman. Simple as that.'

Mark shook his head in disbelief. Here was this young man volunteering to do something good for his community. It shook him and out of nowhere he asked how you joined the police. The young man, Robert was his name Mark learned, raised his eyebrows and suggested Mark have a word with the station HR man. He was introduced and the HR man handed him a sheaf of papers detailing the various routes into the police force. Somehow Mark knew his life was about to take a new direction.

It turned out he needed to go to school, well to adult education classes, to get five GCSE's including English and mathematics. Mark already had Polish qualifications that exceeded the English equivalents but, as it turned out, they couldn't be used in lieu of the English qualifications. So, he started attending night school and within a year he had the qualifications needed to join the police as a recruit doing a two-year course.

It wasn't long before he was noticed by the upper echelons in the force who had him picked out for special duties. Mark was physically tough from the years spent on the fishing boat, he spoke

Polish and passable German as well as the English he had learned, and he was Jewish, if not practicing. The force had been under fire for a number of anti-Semitic remarks by some of its officers and the Assistant Chief Constable saw promoting Mark as going some way to silencing the criticisms.

It took him a few years and a few more exams but eventually he became a full constable with special duties giving school and community talks and a remit to educate the public on tolerance in the community. He liked the work, liked the respect he got from the force and he liked the fact he was giving something back to this community that had welcomed him into their city. From Hull he was seconded to Southampton and the Hampshire and Isle of Wight police force and although Hull had been good to him, he decided to stay in Southampton.

V

It was in Southampton he met Maryja. He had found digs in Portswood and while exploring the neighbourhood had wandered across Cobden Bridge to Bitterne. He followed the main road running beside the Itchen River and was surprised to come across a Polish delicatessen. He went in and after gathering up a few items went to the cashier. A bright eyed petite blond smiled at him and so he asked her in Polish if they had any kielbasa. He didn't really want any but couldn't think of what else to say. 'She smiled and called out to the back room for her uncle to come out. 'Sorry', she said, 'I don't speak that much Polish.' Mark smiled back. 'That's OK. I didn't feel like sausage today anyway.'

He kept going in every day or two to do his shopping hoping to find the bright-eyed girl on the till again. He learnt her name was Mary, 'Maryja, if you ask my mother or father', she said. 'But normally just Mary here.' Eventually he plucked up enough courage to ask her out to dinner. He was surprised when she said 'yes' though somehow he thought it would all work out. It did. Within a month he had proposed to her and while she said 'yes, really, really yes', she also said they ought to see her parents and get their permission.

Mary's parents had retired to the Isle of Wight just across the water, so the next weekend Mark and Mary boarded the ferry for the short ride across to the island. They drove to Ventnor where Mary's parents rented a house and were warmly greeted by her mother and father. It was almost as if they couldn't believe their daughter's luck: A Polish lad washed up on the shores of England and now a policeman wanted to marry their daughter. There was a lot of hugging and kissing and a definite enthusiasm for the idea of Mark and Mary getting married.

There was little dispute the wedding would be in St Catherine's in Ventnor where Mary's parents lived. As Mark trundled back and forth organising the wedding he started to feel an intimacy with the island and the people who lived there after the dark streets of Hull.

It didn't take long for him to link this fellowship with living and working on the island, so he applied to his station manager for a permanent transfer to the Isle of Wight. The idea of living on an island and still being part of the country that had adopted him had an appeal he couldn't quite put his finger on. An island, separate but connected, peopled by refugees from the mainland who had drifted here for one reason or another or for no reason at all. And the local population born and bred here that seemed almost like a native tribe. Caulkheads they were called. The idea of living here intrigued him. There was alchemy at work.

Mark and Mary soon settled down on the Isle of Wight. At first, they lived in a rented house close to the river in Newport. Although Mary wanted a child it soon became apparent after numerous visits to the hospital that was not going to happen. Still they were content with their life on the island and planned to buy a house in Shalfleet just up from Newtown Creek.

The island was a mixture of people from different walks of life and different sub-cultures. There were the caulkheads who had lived on the island for generations. There were the 'oveners' who had come over from the big island to live here. And there were the wealthy second home owners with good jobs, nearly always, it seemed, something to do with financial services Mark discovered, who came over on weekends and school holidays. And around Cowes and Yarmouth there was the yachting set and their chichi clubs. Mark discovered that the island was not some peaceful idyll divorced from the ills of the mainland. It had its share of poverty, domestic violence, burglaries, even the odd murder, but in essence the crime figures were lower than the mainland and the island was a comparative haven of peace.

Mark rose through the ranks to become the lead detective inspector on the island. Soon he was earning enough for them to buy a cottage in Shalfleet just up from Newtown Creek. Mark and Mary would often walk down to where the creek opened out to an estuary popular with cruising yachts visiting the island. For them it was a bucolic paradise that they hoped to reture to in the future.

They had twenty contented years before Mary was diagnosed with breast cancer. Mark was devastated and took as much time off as he could to be with Mary. The plan to retire to Shalfleet went out the window as Mark cared for Mary in her last days. As she deteriorated Mark decided to retire early from the police and spend his time caring for her.

vi

After Mary died Mark sold the house and moved into a chalet in Gurnard Pines. He owed money on the mortgage for the house and had needed to sell it. More than that he couldn't live in their house, the house they had picked out together. It seemed wrong to Mark that he should live there when his heart had been pierced by the creeping disease that had killed his wife.

He had a small pension from the police and did a few gardening jobs on the side to bring in a little extra and keep himself fit and distracted. He had thought about rejoining the police force but decided his heart wasn't in it after Mary's death. Now he had this letter from the Assistant Chief Constable offering him an interim position as the lead investigator on this old case he had investigated a while ago when life on the island offered him everything he thought he needed. And they were prepared to pay him well including expenses. God knows he needed it.

He rang Southampton central police station and was surprised to be put through straight away to the Assistant Chief Constable who greeted him warmly and said he was happy Mark wanted to take over the investigation. The unsolved homicide, likely murder, and the missing person case needed wrapping up the Assistant Chief Constable said. Mark would need to come to Southampton to fill in a few forms and undergo a medical but for now he would send over the case details. It was a cold case that Mark had investigated some ten years previously and apparently new information on the case had turned up. That included a body wrapped in burlap that had been found in the mud at Newtown Creek.

Mark dredged his memory for the details of the case. It had involved the daughter of a millionaire called Bridgewater and she had been killed, probably murdered, down in the marina at Cowes. There was the partner of the woman who had skippered Bridgewater's yacht. He had been cleared of the murder, though not by the media or her father. He had disappeared later off his yacht though that was filed as death by misadventure even though no body had been found. The case had never been solved and Mark regretted that he had not solved the case. Perhaps now new information had come to light he could make ammends. No doubt he would learn what the new information was when the files arrived and the body had been examined by the coroner.

Mark was duly signed back into the force in Southampton and set about reacquainting himself with the force headquarters on the Isle of Wight and reading through the files. The new body that had been found half buried in the mud in Newtown Creek was much decomposed after lying there for some time and was still with the coroner in Southampton. Mark now needed to interview the original witnesses and go back over the case until the coroner's report came in.

vii

Mark started off with a list of witnesses he wanted to interview.

Teddy Bilkman or Jackson, who now goes by the name of Freddy. Mark remembered the case, one of his first on the island, of the young teenager done for drugs and he remembers too his violence when he arrested him. He appears to have straightened himself out and done well for himself in the catering trade and with a share in a gastropub in Cowes.

Sebastian Phillips, the son of a banker and crew on Bridgewater's yacht who was reported to have had an argument with Sophie Bridgewater just before her death and an altercation with Ted/Freddy Jackson around the same time.

George Phillips, the father of Sebastian who swore his son was with him at the Yacht Squadron at the time of Sophie's death. He was reported to be annoyed at the election and presence of Bridgewater in the Squadron and had been upset when his son had been kicked off Bridgewater's yacht by the daughter.

Susie Amato, the girlfriend and partner of Ted/Freddy. She had been miffed about Ted/Freddy's close relationship to Sophie Bridgewater and the couple had apparently argued about Ted/Freddy's friendship with Bridgewater's daughter.

Stephen Bridgewater, the disgraced father of Sophie Bridgewater. He was a self-made millionaire on the back of a publishing and real estate empire that after the murder of his daughter turned out to be a pack of cards that came tumbling down. His overstretched bank loans and the exposure of his extensive interests in porn publishing had caused major backers to pull out of his various businesses and his fortune imploded.

Mick Waterstone, the boatyard owner where Emile has built his yacht and also to whom he had gifted her when he went missing, presumed dead.

Emile Jefferson, the partner of Sophie Bridgewater and initial suspect. He was presumed dead after a boating accident in Newtown Creek.

After reading through the old paperwork for the case Mark felt a certain nostalgia for those early days on the island. He and Mary had been happy, planning their future life here, going out to the local pubs and taking long walks around the coast and along the beaches scattered around the island.

Now he felt not just nostalgia but a dark melancholy he had been robbed of life and an anger at the injustice of it all. He lit a cigarette remembering Mary's antipathy to the habit. He had given up years ago but now he didn't care even if he could hear Mary's gentle chiding in the background.

viii

Mark booked a table down at Ted/Freddy's gastropub, the Boathouse, in Cowes. He wanted to get a feel for the place, for Cowes and Ted/Freddy. He was conscious he was the only single person in the pub but sat down at his table in the back of the restaurant and picked up the menu. He wasn't really hungry but wanted a bit of time to look around. Even after all these years he recognised Ted/Freddy hovering behind the bar and occasionally disappearing into the kitchen. He had got a little chubbier than in his youth and there was a touch of grey in his hair, but he was still recognisable.

Mark rang Ted/Freddy the next day to ask him to come down to the station. 'Just to clear things up: Are you Ted or Freddy these days?' Mark asked him. 'And by the way this is purely routine covering an old case. I'll explain everything when you are here.'

Freddy, that was what he liked to be called these days Mark learnt, turned up at the police station the next day. He explained that when he used his brother's name to call his business 'Freddy's Posh Nosh' that everyone assumed his name was Freddy. Mark suggested he call him Freddy but for the paperwork would use his given name.

'Freddy, if I can call you by your Christian name, I'm looking at an old case concerning the death of Sophie Bridgewater some fifteen years ago. Nothing to worry about here but I need to go over a few details. By the way, you don't remember me, do you?'

Freddy looked puzzled and shook his head while scrutinizing Mark. Then he nodded. 'I remember you from the time when Sophie was killed. You were on the case though I didn't talk to you then.'

Mark smiled. 'We go way back before that Freddy… to when you were still Teddy. I was the arresting officer when you cut loose on the quay in Newport, beat up the guy in the gang and got caught with class A drugs on you. I was the one who suggested you do some of the qualifications they teach at the Young Offenders Prison. Remember?'

Freddy nodded. 'I do remember you now. You treated me decently - not something I expected from a copper. And you got me on those courses in Parkhurst. But I haven't done anything since then except build up my business. In fact, I remember now – you were in the restaurant the other day. What did you have? Was it any good?'

Mark smiled. 'Venison and red wine pie. It was very good. You have done well since those early days, but we need to get back to the case of Sophie Bridgewater.' Mark shuffled the files in front of him then looked intently at Freddy. 'Before Sophie Bridgewater was killed you had an argument with her and with one of her crew, a Sebastian Phillips. Witnesses have said you grabbed him by the throat and threw him down on the pontoon. Is that correct?'

Freddy sighed. 'I was reacting to him trying to hit me. He attacked me first and I responded and put him down. He had been ranting and raving at Sophie because she had just sacked him from the crew on the yacht. I didn't see him after that though his father did come around to the shop where we made the lunch boxes and threaten to take legal action against me. He didn't.'

Mark nodded. 'This much I know but I do see a certain similarity between the attack on Sebastian and your attack on the lad in Newport. And an examination of Sophie determined that she had bruises on her neck and back before going in the water. You see where I am going?'

Freddy nodded and then sat up straight. 'I can see what you are trying to do but I had nothing to do with Sophie's death. On the contrary I was her friend. I looked after her that's why I had the to-do with the Sebastian fellow. I went down there during the storm because I was worried...' Freddy tailed off his angry reply realising what he was saying and looked at Mark with downcast eyes.

ix

Mark tapped the papers on his desk. 'So, you were down in the marina? That's not in the notes I have here.' He looked intently at Freddy. 'What were you doing down there?'

'I wasn't down at the boats' Freddy said. 'I just went down to the quay to see what was going on in the storm. I mean I couldn't take any lunchbox orders in that weather – could I? And I just wanted to make sure Sophie's boat was OK. But I didn't go down to it. If you are trying to say I had something to do with this it just isn't true. I went down to the marina quay, looked at the boats for ten minutes or so and then came back here.'

Mark shuffled the papers on his desk again. 'Did anyone see you down there?' he asked. 'And why didn't you mention this when you were interviewed?'

Freddy shook his head. 'I suppose I was worried I would be dobbed in because I had argued with Sophie and floored the Sebastian guy. I'm not sure really.' He looked at the floor and gestured towards Mark with his hands outstretched. 'You know very well guys like me are always the ones you coppers suspect of wrongdoing. I mean I still have a record, don't I? Doesn't matter that I cleaned up my act and set up a successful business. Bought this pub and restaurant. All that doesn't matter to you lot. But I really didn't do anything. Never saw Sophie or anyone else down there. So, unless you have some sort of proof, I'll be off. I've got a restaurant to run.'

Mark nodded. He really wasn't sure of what to make of this but decided to let Freddy go. 'Just remember to stay on the island' he said. 'I may have to call you in again. And I need to talk to your partner Susie Amato.'

X

The autopsy report on the body arrived on Mark's desk the next day. In lots of ways it would have answered a lot of questions if it was Emile's body. It wasn't. The body, or what was left of it, was probably a person who had been buried at sea off the Needles on the western end of the island and somehow been washed by winter storms over a number of years into the mud at Newtown Creek. The coroner had confirmed the DNA from the body did not match the sample Emile had given during the inquest into the death of Sophie.

Over the next few days Mark interviewed some of the other people on his list. Sebastian arrived with his father and a solicitor. There was little to take from the interview apart from the father and son exuding an apparent contempt for being called into the police station for the interview. Sebastian the son had been at the Squadron with his father and at least a dozen witnesses. So the solicitor claimed. The interview was soon over and they departed with the solicitor suggesting that Mark should leave his clients alone and maybe look elsewhere for a guilty party.

He decided to call in Freddy's partner or girlfriend or companion. Susie Amato worked in the kitchen of The Boathouse pub and had been with Freddy for quite a while now. Mark had noticed that the police had been called to a domestic incident at Freddy's Posh Nosh the day after Sophie's death, but no charges had been made. When Susie walked in Mark offered tea or coffee to her which was politely declined.

'Sorry detective' she said. 'I'm quite picky about my tea and coffee and I doubt yours is to my taste.'

Mark grimaced a little and looked at his notes. 'I see you and Freddy had some sort of argument the day after Sophie's death. Can you tell me what that was about?'

Susie's mouth tightened. 'I don't really see what this has to do with this retrospective on Sophie's death. In fact, I'm wondering why you would bring this up at all. It was a private matter between me and Freddy and possibly a bit much wine on both our parts.'

Mark sighed. 'Look, I apologise for asking but I am just trying to get to the bottom of this old case and so far I'm not getting anywhere. So, anything that might point me in the right direction would be useful.'

Susie looked at Mark and nodded. 'OK. We were arguing about Sophie. I was a bit, no a lot, pissed off that he had been seeing her down on the pontoon and then when she switched him out of the equation, he was pretty angry. Kept going on about Sophie. So, I got angry and the next thing he shoves me out the door and tells me not to come back. Of course, he opened it a minute or two later and I came back in. I don't know who called the cops. Look I can tell you Freddy didn't do anything. And by the way we have been happily together for a lot of years now. I was there from the beginning you know.'

Mark looked at his papers, at Susie, and smiled. She seemed quite open about what had happened and with her life now. Freddy on the other hand had said nothing about the tiff with Susie after his argument with Sophie and Mark made a mental note to talk to Freddy about this later.

xi

Mark wondered who to interview next. He didn't seem to be making much headway with the cold case and he knew he would have to report back to the Assistant Chief Constable soon on progress on the case. He wondered if the force would drop the case now the body that had washed up proved not to be Emile. He wasn't sure where to go so he decided to get on with interviewing some minor witnesses.

He called up Mick's yard where Emile had built his yacht and made an appointment to see him down at his boatyard on the Medina River. When he got there Mick greeted him warmly and invited him to sit with him. 'Tea?' Mick asked.

And without waiting for a reply put the kettle on. 'How do you take your tea?' he asked.

Mark sat on the chair outside the boatshed and watched the river. The tide was ebbing against the wind blowing upstream so there was a fair chop on the water and the boats on Mick's bit of quay were bobbing gently in the water. He wondered which yacht was the one Emile had built and as he understood it, then gifted it to Mick in the note he had left on board in Newtown Creek.

Mick emerged with two mugs of tea and handed one of them to Mark. 'Didn't know what you had in your tea, so I put a bit of both in' he said. Mick gazed out over the water before saying anything. 'You know Em and I used to sit here with a beer and a fag after work. Didn't talk much. Just small talk really. Em was never much of a talker anyway. What do you want to know? Everyone knows by now you are looking at that old case of Sophie Bridgewater.'

Mark wasn't too sure of what he needed to know from Mick but started in with the obvious. 'So why do you think Emile gifted the boat to you. I mean it must have been worth a bit of money.'

Mick pursed his lips. 'I don't really think of it as mine. I'm more like the custodian of that boat. Em put his heart and soul into building it and I sort of feel, not for any reason mind you, that I am just looking after it until Em gets back to me. I miss that big old bear of a man. We were good friends.'

Mark smiled. Mick had a forlorn look to him as if Emile had deserted him needlessly. 'Do you think he is still alive?' Mark asked. 'I mean do you think he just disappeared somehow from the boat?'

Mick chuckled. 'I really don't know but I do know what you are trying to get me to say. I've spent a long time thinking and wondering about him and I truthfully don't know. I do find it odd that he might have accidentally gone overboard and drowned or something like that. Maybe he hit his head on something and toppled overboard. It happens. But on the other hand, Em was always so careful and after all those miles he had sailed I just find it unlikely. Do you want to see *Selene* – his boat?'

Mick didn't wait for a reply but motioned to Mark to follow him into the shed. 'She is hauled out now for a few little boat jobs but essentially this is the boat Em left behind.'

Mark knew nothing about boats but Em's boat, the late Em's boat, was like a sculpture in wood. The boat was shaped for the water with wonderful sinuous curves to the hull. The cabin was varnished mahogany with three oval portholes along its length. Momentarily it took his breath away. He turned to Mick.

'If Emile did fall overboard how would he get back on board? That is assuming he was sailing alone.'

Mick took Mark around to the transom and pointed out the chocks on either side of the rudder. 'You can climb up the rudder to the bumpkin, that triangular affair sticking out, and so up onto the deck. It's a bit of an effort but doable and Em was reasonably fit... well apart from the continuous cough he had. I put it down to all the teak dust. Mind you he was a bit of a smoker.'

Mark continued gazing at the boat. It really was a work of art, almost a living thing and he thought he could see it cleaving the waves as the sails pulled it along. 'Can I take a peep inside?' he asked Mick who nodded and went off to get a ladder. The interior of *Selene* was like being inside a beautiful piece of cabinetwork. The woodwork inside was minimal but what there was reflected a love of wood and the hand of an artisan. The mahogany glowed in the half-light the portholes let in and the saloon table had an exquisite marquetry inlaid compass rose in different woods.

Mark almost held his breath as he took in the interior. How had so much, a small galley, a heads, a double bunk in the forepeak and saloon berths in moss green velvet, all been squeezed so beautifully into this small space. He looked at Mick sitting in the cockpit and watched him brush away a tear.

Mark climbed out of the companionway to sit in the cockpit. He looked at Mick and asked him the question that had been on his mind as he looked around the interior of *Selene*. 'Mick. What is the photo of another yacht doing on the bulkhead? Did it belong to Emile?'

Mick hesitated before replying. 'Yes, it did. A boat he called *Seven Tenths* after the extent of the oceans on the planet. He kept it in Southampton somewhere though I'm not sure exactly where. He never said. I know he sailed off down to the Mediterranean for a while before he came back here and started building *Selene*. I think he sold it years ago when he started building this boat, but I really don't know for sure.'

Mark raised his eyebrows and looked at Mick. 'You really don't know where he used to keep this boat? Is it possible to find out?'

Mick looked sidelong at Mark. 'Look… you are the police so you must be able to find out these things. You have to understand Em didn't talk very much about himself or the events in his life. We mostly just made small talk about this or that, about boatbuilding and stuff like that. The only topic you could get Em talking about was the sea and sailing on it. He was wedded to the sea, to the weather and how you coped with it at sea, to anything that was to do with his love of the sea. For a boy from the wastelands of Essex he somehow had salt in his veins.

The only other thing that he sometimes talked about was Sophie and her father and how angry he was about his loss and the fact that Bridgewater somehow blamed him for her death and his downfall. It niggled him.'

X

It didn't take too long for Mark to get Southampton checking for the whereabouts of

Emile's old boat. He had the name, *Seven Tenths*, and Mick had told him he thought the manufacturer was Beneteau Yachts. Central in Southampton came up with a boat that had been kept in the Itchen that roughly matched the description, a Beneteau 36, that had been called *Seven Tenths* and was owned by a Miles James. Mark smiled when he read the name of the owner. Emile James Jefferson still likely owned the boat under the variation on his name of Miles James.

The Southampton force had sent a man around to check on the boat without success. The owner of the moorings on the Itchen told him that the boat hadn't been there for years and he had no idea where it was now. Mark was not surprised but now at last he had a lead to go on. He put out a general request to the police and the coastguard to be on the lookout for the yacht though in truth he didn't hold out much hope of a response. The police and the coastguard were overstretched already and probably had little time to deal with a request like his.

Mark still had one witness to track down and that was proving more difficult than he thought. Stephen Bridgewater had taken to the bottle after his business empire had crumbled into nothing. His wife and younger daughter had left him and he had seemingly disappeared without further ado. He was able to track down the wife, Bridget Bridgewater and the daughter Chloe.

He rang the wife first who asked him what he wanted. By law he had to say he was with the Hampshire and Isle of Wight Police at which she muttered 'Don't ring me again' and put the phone down. Chloe the daughter gave him much the same response but with a lot more invective. He thought about bringing them in for questioning but was dubious about what he might learn and indeed what they actually knew about the whereabouts of Stephen Bridgewater. From the records he had it seemed they had distanced themselves as far as they could from him.

Mark shuffled through the papers and reports in the file. Something niggled at the back of his mind about Bridgewater and his companies. It took a while as he shuffled through the company records before it clicked. Bridgewater's photographer from the early days, Grigsby, had retired and bought a house in France through one of Bridgewater's companies. He looked at the date. Fifteen years ago. Then he made a call to the station for them to locate Evan Grigsby.

It didn't take long for them to get back to say Evan Grigsby had died ten years ago. Mark pulled out the file on the house sale and located the address on Google. It was a smallholding near a village just outside Dinan in Brittany. Mark scribbled down the address and sat back with a cigarette to think over the plan that was forming in his head. A madcap plan for someone like him.

xii

Mark was never sure where or why he got this notion in his head that he should visit the house in France. Ever since he had defected from the fishing boat in Hull, he had never left England to journey anywhere. Really most of his life had centred around the Isle of Wight and he had felt no inclination to travel outside his adopted country. Even when Poland had extracted itself from the iron fist of communism, he had no desire to travel back there, to see what had happened to the country he was born into, see where he had grown up, contemplate the place he had left.

He knew that the Hampshire and Isle of Wight force wouldn't sanction him visiting France and, in any case,, he had no jurisdiction there. He would have to visit as a private citizen. He didn't have any travel plans and it took a while until he found his passport. He sat down and scribbled a list of what he needed to do to get to France and then phoned in to say he was taking a break for a bit. Surprisingly that seemed to go down OK.

He surprised himself on how organised he was with just a few days to plan everything. He booked a ticket on the Portsmouth to St Malo ferry and arranged a hire car and a hotel for when he arrived. Three days later he found himself boarding the ferry at Portsmouth for the overnight trip to St Malo. On the ferry he reflected on the fact that Mary had really done all the planning in their life. He smiled to himself. He was sure she would be proud of him setting off on a hunch, a whim, on an almost spontaneous leap into the unknown. Somehow, he felt he might be emerging from the darkness that had enveloped him after Mary's death.

He slept well on the ferry as it rolled across a stormy Channel night. It brought back memories of the trawler he had worked on out of Gdansk though not bad memories, more flashes of a life long ago. The ferry docked in St Malo in the early morning and he walked down the ramp to find a young woman holding a cardboard sign with his name on it. She showed him to the hire car, got him to sign some paperwork and handed him the keys. He had taken the trouble to load the route to Dinan on his phone and set off for the town through the rush hour traffic in St Malo. So far so good.

Mark arrived at the small hotel he had booked close to the river that runs through Dinan. Le

Poisson Ivre was not the sort of place he would normally stay in, but it served a purpose that lurked in the back of his head – it overlooked the river and the quayed area of Port de Dinan. Once he had booked in he wandered down to a café on the riverside and contemplated the view. Yachts were tied up along the quay and several had owners busy working on board. When he had finished his coffee, he walked down to the quay and greeted the first person on a yacht that he came across. Given he spoke little or no French he had researched a few phrases beforehand.

'Parles-tu Anglais?' Mark asked. The man looked quizzically at him and then shouted down the quay to another working on a yacht. He then motioned Mark to go along to him.

'You are English?' the man asked. Mark nodded. 'So, what do you want on this fine morning in Brittany?'

Mark thanked him for taking the time to talk to him. 'I'm looking for a friend, an English friend, whose yacht might be here' Mark said. It's a

Beneteau 36 from 1990 and is, or was, called *Seven Tenths*. Do you know if it is here?'

The man on the yacht eyed him suspiciously for a minute before replying. 'So what has he done? This friend of yours. What did you say his name was?'

'I didn't' Mark said. 'But it's Emile Jefferson and he hasn't done anything wrong. I can show you a picture of a Beneteau 36 if you like.' Mark pulled out his phone but the man waved it away.

'I know what an old Beneteau 36 looks like' he said. He seemed to be sizing things up before he replied. 'Your friend's boat is on a mooring off Plouer sur Rance downriver from here. But I doubt he is on it – I haven't seen him around for months. And by the way I can sort of smell that you are a policeman or something similar. If he was around here, trust me, I wouldn't tell you.'

Mark grinned. It must be the way I stand he thought. Or the way I talk. Anyway, not to worry as he didn't have any way to get out to a mooring and if there was no-one on the boat there was no point anyway. He just needed confirmation the boat was here as he had half-suspected.

He ate well in the restaurant at the hotel. He had never really been that interested in food. To him it was just fuel. But the meal here was something of a revelation to him. He just wished Mary was here with him.

xi

The house that Grigsby had bought through Bridgewater's company was near a little village called Saint James a few kilometres outside Dinan. As he drove to the village Mark didn't really have a clear idea of what he was going to do there. He thought that maybe he would go into the village and park near a bar or a grocery shop and see if Bridgewater or Emile turned up. It was, he admitted to himself, a somewhat silly plan when he had the exact address of the house Grigsby had bought, though of course he didn't know if had been sold on since then. Still: clutching at straws and all that he thought.

In Saint James he went into the Sports Café and nursed a cup of coffee for an hour or so. This at least gave him time to pluck up the courage to drive back down the road and take the rough track that his phone told him lead to the approximate location of the house. He duly turned off down a gravel road and soon came to an old Maison d'Maitre at the end. He stopped the car and sat there for a bit wondering what to do next. He didn't have to wait long before the front door opened and a gaunt figure emerged.

Mark only barely recognised Emile. The figure at the door looked years older, his bushy beard unkempt and his body bent like an old man. What Mark did notice was that he was cradling a shotgun. He got out of the car and spread his hands wide.
'I'm unarmed' he said. 'You don't need that.'

Emile grimaced and looked confused. He coughed, a great hacking cough that racked his body and caused him to double over even further. He smiled, at least Mark took it for a smile, and motioned Mark over. 'Would you like a cup of tea?' he asked. 'And by the way it's not loaded.'

Mark put his arms down to his side and walked slowly over to the house. He was still worried about the shotgun Emile had but somehow, he sensed that it wouldn't be used. At least that was what he hoped. Emile turned and walked inside. Mark followed into a great hall and a large modern kitchen off it. Emile put the gun on the table and went to the sink to fill a kettle before plugging it in and turning it on.

Emile turned to Mark. 'I figured someone would come sooner or later' he said. 'But I didn't expect it to be you. I thought it would be the local gendarme. By the way how do you take your tea?'

Mark told him and watched as he shuffled over to the fridge. Halfway across he started coughing again and pulled out a wad of paper towel to hack into. It didn't look good. 'Are you alright? Mark asked.

Emile got the milk out of the fridge and put it on the table. 'What do you think? Do I look alright to you? In any case ask the question that must be on your mind.'

Mark stirred some sugar into the mug. 'OK. So is Bridgewater here?'

Emile smiled that lopsided grimace again that passed for a smile. 'He is out the back. In the vegetable garden. I'd like to say six foot under, but I didn't have the strength to dig that far so I'd say one foot under.' He looked directly at Mark. 'And yes. I shot him with that gun there. He deserved it for what he did to all of us but especially to Sophie. He was the one that killed her. Maybe it was accidental… maybe not.' He looked at Mark to see whether what he had just said registered. 'Just kidding. Well sort of. Sit down and drink your tea and I'll tell you what happened.'

xii

Mark took a gulp of his tea and wondered where to start. He knew he would have to get in touch with the gendarmerie in Dinan, but first he had the feeling that Emile needed to tell him what had happened. And he needed to hear what the story was. 'So what happened?' Mark asked. It was a weak way to start but he couldn't think of anything else.

Emile nursed his tea and contemplated this man who had walked into his life. He knew that the police would arrive at some time so he might as well tell him what he knew, or at least what he supposed as well as how it all arrived at this.

'What is your name?' Emile asked. 'I do remember you vaguely from long ago, but not with any clarity. Not that much has clarity anymore. As you may have guessed I slipped off *Selene* in the dark and paddled ashore on an old surfboard I had. I threw that into the marsh knowing no-one would imagine it was anything but an old abandoned bit of debris. After that I hiked up to the main road and retrieved a bicycle I had left there and cycled into Cowes and down to Mick's yard. I suppose he was an accomplice in all this but it really doesn't matter anymore.

Mick took me over to Southampton on a little motorboat he was fixing up and I guess you have worked out already that I still had my old Beneteau over there that I got out to. Really no-one ever notices anything if you look like you know what you are doing.'

Mark interrupted. 'So how did you know where Bridgewater was?'

Emile smiled that lop-sided grimace of his before lapsing into another coughing fit. He pulled a rag of a handkerchief from his pocket and Mark could see it was spotted with blood. 'He, I mean Bridgewater, had told me about the house over here and how he bought it in his photographer's name. I had met Grigsby a few times when he came over to Cowes. He didn't like sailing, but he did like the parties. So anyway, Bridgewater said I could use it anytime I wanted to. Take Sophie over there. Have a break in France. I never did but I did know where the house was… Is.' He coughed again.

'I sailed *Seven Tenths* over here… pretty easy trip really. Sailed into Saint Malo and up to the Rance. Put the boat on a mooring and cadged a trip ashore with my backpack. I didn't really know if Bridgewater would be here, but I suspected he was. After his empire came down around his ears he disappeared and where would he go to except here. When he opened the front door I expected him to tell me to 'fuck off'… but he didn't. After all those years I think he wanted to come clean about the whole affair and what better person than me, the person he had blamed for Sophie's death and then driven me out of the life I had. He invited me in.'

Mark looked at him and nodded for him to go on. The story was an odd one but he sensed it was mostly true. And he was curious about what came next.

Emile started but was interrupted by a coughing fit. He cleared his throat and tried again. 'There I was sitting at this table just like you are sitting there now, drinking tea and talking as if nothing untoward had happened in our past. In many ways we were two lonely souls that only connected over that one incident all those years ago. As if somehow we could find redemption talking about it in a farmhouse in France. It was madness of course and who is to say which of us was more off kilter than the other. You know he did it don't you?' Emile looked at Mark and furrowed his brow.

This caught Mark unawares. As far as he knew Stephen Bridgewater had been at home when Sophie died. At least that was what his wife and daughter had said if he remembered the interview notes correctly. Then he remembered their aggressive attitude when he had phoned. Perhaps he should have pressed them further. 'Tell me about it' Mark said.

'I was sitting here when Bridgewater excused himself. Said he wouldn't be a moment. When he came back in he was holding that same shotgun there. Pointed it at me and said that I was obviously here because I'd worked out what had happened. I protested but it didn't make any difference. He just pointed it at me and then asked how I had worked out what had happened with Sophie. He told me it was an accident and he hadn't intended to harm her. He was down on the pontoon arguing with her and telling her she would get nothing if she ever betrayed his confidence and talked about his business empire.

She had argued back. 'Always was a devious little bitch even if she was my daughter' he told me. 'I grabbed her to shake some sense into her and somehow while we struggled, she slipped and caught her foot on a mooring cleat on the pontoon and fell into the water.'

Emile looked at Mark and was nearly in tears at this stage. 'So now he told me he would have to dispose of me since I had worked out what had happened. Reckoned no one would miss me anyway. I thought it was the end and then he simply tucked the muzzle under his chin and pulled the trigger. Scared the shit out of me. There was blood everywhere and bits of the back of his head all over the kitchen. I suppose he had lived with the guilt of it for so long that it had eaten into him and I suppose he might have been going to commit suicide for a while. Who knows?'

Mark shook his head. 'So why didn't you report this to the gendarmerie? If this is what happened. After all it was not your fault. Or was it?'

Emile shrugged. 'I guess I wasn't worried about anything. You have probably noticed I'm not in the best health. In fact, I probably haven't got long left. I thought I'd just bury him out the back in the vegetable garden and stay here for a bit. I cleaned up as best I could, but you can still see stains on the floor and walls. It was a shit-show of a mess. And now you have turned up and I guess you will want to get in touch with the police here. So be it. I'm done now Bridgewater is gone.'

Mark sighed. He wasn't too sure about Emile's account of what had happened. As he pondered the story Emile had told him it occurred to him that he hadn't checked the shotgun on the table to see if was loaded or not. Normal police practice that you were taught from day one. Still Emile hadn't looked like he was going to use it, so Mark hoped it was in fact not loaded. One way to find out he thought. Call the Gendarmerie in Dinan to send someone out here. He pulled out his phone and punched in 17. At least he had looked that up before catching the ferry over to France.

The gendarme arrived an hour later. He was a young recruit who had obviously been told to go and placate 'Les Anglais'. When he walked into the room and saw the shotgun on the table his hand immediately went to his holster. Mark said an abrupt 'Non' and pulled out his warrant card and handed it to the gendarme. Still the gendarme moved quickly to pluck the shotgun off the table, break it open only to find it empty and then prop it in the corner. He relaxed and asked Mark a question in rapid French. Mark looked flustered and mumbled to the gendarme that he didn't speak French. The young gendarme smiled and pulled out his phone and dialed a number before talking excitedly to someone on the other end. The main station Mark assumed.

It took only minutes for two police cars, blue lights flashing, to pull up outside and disgorge four gendarmes. One of them had a flak jacket and carried an automatic rifle. They marched into the kitchen and after a short conversation with the young gendarme and a brief inspection of Mark's warrant card asked Mark and Emile to go with them to the station in Dinan.

xiii

Mark and Emile were escorted into an office in the Gendarmerie in Dinan where an older officer sat behind his desk. He addressed them in perfect English and pointed to Emile. 'You are not very well my officers tell me, so I think the best thing is to get you up to the hospital to see what is wrong. And of course, if we can fix it.' He smiled, a kindly smile, at Emile and then motioned for one of his gendarmes to take Emile out.

After that he turned to Mark. 'You know you are not in your jurisdiction here. I'm sure you know that so perhaps you could tell me why you are here and why you called us. I believe you may also have something to say about your friend and, if I am not mistaken, the other man who was living there. Yes, we do know that your friend is not the owner of the house. That was a …' He brought up a register on his screen and scrolled down. 'Ah yes. A Stephen Bridgewater who registered with the town council a few years ago. Not that we have had any trouble from him.'

Mark wondered where to start. Maybe the cold case from the island. As best he could he retraced the case and his curious desire to go off-piste and get himself over to France. He explained to the officer that he hadn't actually got permission to come over. Partly he thought, because he had no idea what he would find. It was just a hunch. Quite out of character for him.

The officer seemed somewhat amused at Mark going out of bounds and coming over on his own volition. He was less amused when Mark told him about meeting Emile and that Bridgewater was buried out the back. Suicide Emile had said. He immediately got on the phone and barked out orders. Probably to a forensic unit Mark thought.

'What are we going to do with you now?' the officer asked. Before Mark could reply he answered his own question. 'For the sake of the entente cordial we will let you go but you must stay here in Dinan for a couple of days in case we need to talk to you again. As for your friend that is more difficult. Anyway, we will let you know how he gets on at the hospital. Personally, I don't think he is very well both in his body and his head.'

Mark returned to his hotel near the port in Dinan and went straight to the bar to order a bottle of good red wine. He lit a cigarette and decided he needed to treat himself. Over the next four days he was called into the Gendarmerie a couple of times to firm up on details and answer any new questions. The forensic team had located the shallow grave in the vegetable patch out the back of Bridgewater's house and had formally identified the body from DNA records. The officer who had questioned him - 'My name is Inspecteur Coulange, but you may call me Jean-Guy' – decided after he had taken Mark's address and phone number to let him go on his way. He had smiled at Mark. 'Though if you need to eat and drink well, I can always ask for your return. On business of course but that will involve some good food and drink. However, your friend needs to stay in hospital though the prognosis is not good. The doctors there think he has only a few weeks, maybe a month, to live. Some sort of respiratory disease, I believe, that is quite advanced. I will let you know what happens – never worry.'

Mark was not quite sure why, but it was with a hint of regret that he left Dinan. The ferry back to Portsmouth was straightforward though he did worry what the reaction would be from the central station in Southampton. He rationalised to himself that he had not abused his police powers and that the foray to France was his affair. Still he would have to tell the Assistant Chief Constable in Southampton who had put him on the cold case what he had discovered in France.

On the ferry across to the Isle of Wight he felt a different man to the one who had left only a week or so before. He couldn't explain exactly what it was but somehow he felt lighter in himself and, he reflected, he wasn't too concerned with getting a dressing down from his superior on the case because, after all, he had solved it. Well solved something. He still wasn't sure about Em's account of what had happened.

xiv

Mark soon settled back into life on the island but with a lighter heart than when he had left. He went straight to Mary's grave and sat there for a while relating to her what had happened, how he still missed her, would always miss her, but now he felt there was less bleakness to his life than previously. He told her that too.

He had been back two days when he got a call from Inspector Coulange in Dinan. Emile Jefferson had died that morning. The French inspector hesitated for a moment before continuing. 'Of course, we had to get in touch with the British police and I was put through to your Hampshire and Isle of Wight force. It seems you neglected to tell them you were travelling to France in pursuit of this case. A cold case I believe in which the man who died in our hospital had long been missing and assumed to be dead. Your commander was somewhat taken aback at your presence here, but I did my best to calm your troubled waters. I suspect you will hear from him very soon. In any case do visit us again my friend if you are in need of sustenance.' He chuckled for a minute before hanging up.

The call from the police station in Southampton came a few hours later. Mark was asked to hold before being connected to the Assistant Chief Constable. He didn't mess around with frivolities. 'So, Inspector you pursued this case to France without letting us know your movements and intent. You realise this is a serious offence for a serving officer though as I understand it and the accounts department confirms it, you did this on your account not on police expenses. Is this correct?'

Mark mumbled a reply before clearing his throat and setting out his case in a more confident tone. 'I was following a lead that I really wasn't sure would lead anywhere sir, so I did indeed travel to France at my own expense. I would just add that I used my own resources to track down Emile Fitzgerald and did not liaise with the French until Emile had told me of the goings on France and particularly of the death of Stephen Bridgewater. Emile Jefferson was in no fit state to travel back to the UK and the French inspector placed him in hospital. He is, as I'm sure you have been informed, now deceased of natural causes.'

There was a pause from the Assistant Chief Constable before he replied. 'I really should be giving you a bollocking but here's the thing, off the record you have tied up the loose ends if in a somewhat unorthodox way. What I propose is we keep you on a stipend for any other cases that might require us to employ help on the island. And your slight bending of the rules will not be noted. Case closed.'

For Mark there were still a few things to wrap up. That night he sat down for dinner in the Boathouse. Freddy recognised him straight away and walked over to his table. 'Inspector. You came back. For the food I hope but a bit of news won't go amiss either.' Mark related the bare details to him and assured Freddy that the case was now closed. Freddy smiled. 'By the way the meal is on the house. And more… I do remember your kind words and help when I was arrested all those years ago though it seems like a different life to the one I have now. And you may be happy to hear we are fine and Susie is pregnant. All's well that ends well as my little brother used to say.'

XV

Mark left his visit to Mick last. He didn't tell Mick he was coming but just turned up at the boatyard. There was no one around so he wandered into the shed to look at Emile's boat again. She was buffed and polished and ready to go in the water, the brass shone and the brightwork had been touched up. Mark ran his hand over the topsides feeling the silky curve of the hull. Emile had poured his soul into this boat and Mark felt a tinge of regret that he wasn't here anymore.

He heard a cough behind him and turned to find Mick watching him. 'I see you are admiring the moon goddess' he said. 'She is one of a kind, a testimony to Em. Come and have a beer outside and fill me in on what happened. I did know you were back on the island.'

Mark followed him around to the front of the shed and sat on one of the two rickety chairs with the view out over the river. Mick emerged with two cans and handed one to him. Mark took out a cigarette and wondered how to start. 'You know Em is dead, don't you?' he said. 'He died in a hospital in France a few days ago.'

Mick nodded. 'I'm not surprised. He wasn't that well when he left here. All that dust from cutting and sanding I'd guess. In truth I'm surprised he lasted this long but then he was a tough old bugger.' Mick looked out over the river. 'Still he left behind that testimony to his very being, a work of art that no one can take away from him.' His voice was distant as though he could see Em looking out over the river with him.

Mark was surprised at himself when he next ventured a thought to Mick. 'Perhaps I could come sailing on her if that worked for you. Just a thought and don't be embarrassed to say no.'

Mick looked across to him. 'You ever been on the water before? I mean I don't want you getting seasick or anything like that.'

Mark smiled. 'I worked for two years on a trawler in the North Sea. High seas and bad weather were our constant companions. So no, I don't get seasick.'

Mick smiled. 'I think that would work then. I can soon teach you the basics of sailing, getting those flappy white things to move us along. And I think Em would like that. I mean he would like it that you were sailing on his boat. On *Selene*. We can potter over to Newtown Creek.

Other books from the Taniwha Press UK

www.taniwhapress.com

Sailing Ancient Seas
Rod Heikell
A crippled boat and a lot of broken dreams. A broken marriage and a hunger to sail down into the Indian Ocean. This is both a love story about a boat, his beloved Tetranora and a story of a voyage out of love and into life. Along the way it explores ancient sailing routes from the Mediterranean to the Indian Ocean.

Long hours at the helm gave opportunity to reflect on how those early predecessors managed to arrive safely without the benefit of buoys, lights or binoculars.... an engrossing account of an epic and redemptive voyage. *Cruising Association*

ISBN 978-0-9575849-3-8 Price £10.50 Also in kindle and epub

The Accidental Sailor
Rod Heikell
In 1976 Rod Heikell set off in Roulette, a 20-foot boat that should probably have never left the sheltered waters of the Solent, for the Mediterranean. Via the

French Canals and Biscay, he somehow got to the Mediterranean and sailed to Corsica, Italy and onto Greece. It records the near disasters and highs and lows of a voyage which shaped his life in ways he never imagined. He became the accidental sailor and has led to a life-long love of sailing and exploring the seas. In 1987 he took a Mirror Offshore 18 down the Danube behind the Iron Curtain to the Black Sea and Aegean, probably the longest voyage one these tubby little craft has made.

A cracking read in the tradition of great cruising yarns.
Dick Durham Yachting Monthly

ISBN 978-0-9575849-0-7 Price £9.50   Also in kindle and epub

To Ithaca   J C Graeme
ISBN 978-0-9575849-6-9
Price £6.75 Also in kindle and epub

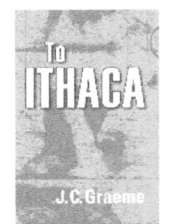

Leaving his orderly, comfortable life Douglas travels to Greece where he becomes embroiled in a dark plot to destroy the manuscript for a book on a secretive neo-Nazi party that his brother has written. On his brother's yacht with the aid of Peter's friends Darcy and Europa he must out-run his pursuers through the Greek islands and try to piece together what is going on. He must also come to terms with his brother and their troubled early years. It is a voyage he is not ready for and one which will change his life.

Fantastic read, drifting between fiction and nonfiction, I did not want the story to end. *Amazon US*

My Name Is No One

**ISBN 978-0-9575849-6-9 Price £6.75
Also in kindle and epub**

If there is a back story to the *Odyssey,* then this novel by J. C. Graeme is it. Forget the return from Troy and a band of heroes voyaging the seas and encountering monsters and adventure aplenty while having their way with the local maidens and the odd goddess. In this story of Odysseus, he is a bar-fly in the Sunset Bar on Khios where he trades stories for jugs of wine with the bar owner Homer. On this adventure he encounters a whole cast of characters and maybe even a goddess or two, though they have little in common with the characters peopling the *Odyssey* as we know it. Some of them may even have been real.

JC Graeme's tongue-in-cheek tale of the voyages of Odysseus is narrated with wit and humour. Many awesome characters and gods from Greek Legends make an appearance but JC Graeme divests them of their pomp and status by portraying them as laymen, which is highly amusing. Odysseus too comes across as a likeable but flawed character. A mediocre sailor, a failed cargo agent, he has also recently run out of the tales from the dockside that bought him his wine in Homer's bar. Middle-aged and strapped for cash, he rashly takes on a sailing delivery trip. With only a smattering of knowledge about the nature of the local winds and coastline, he inevitably gets lost – for years - sailing to many strange places, and meeting people who all seem to conspire to delay his return home.

ISBN 978-0-9575849-9-0 Price £7.50   Also in kindle and epub

Crab's Odyssey: Malta to Istanbul in an Open Boat

Penny Minney

In the wake of the tales of George Millar in Isabel and the Sea and Ernle Bradford in The Journeying Moon sailing through the Mediterranean after World War II comes Penny Minney's Crab's Odyssey recounting the adventures of a group of undergraduates sailing a 17-foot ship's lifeboat from Malta to Istanbul in the 1950's.

It began with the shipwreck of the ferry taking them to join their newly purchased boat in Malta and ended with them finding an authoritative Ancient Greek historian wrong about the Bosporus passage. In the 1950s, two ordinary second-year students at Somerville College Oxford and their assorted crews sailed more than 1,500 miles in an open boat over four summers.

Joining them at different junctures was a medley of fellow-sailors. To pick up crew at a pre-arranged rendezvous at fortnightly intervals was a juggling act that for one crew member took three nights, eight trains and a ferry. But they only mislaid one – and in the search came close to losing the skipper.

There were no plans for a journey to Istanbul at the outset, but the further they sailed, the more their ambitions grew. There were six major crossings – often with non-stop baling – and much coast-hopping. Tensions on board, unexpected gifts and encounters, and an unexpected proposal: the book vividly recalls a Mediterranean Europe emerging from WWII.

ISBN 978-09954699-2-1 £10.50

THE GIFT OF A SEA

A Short History of Yachting in the Mediterranean

Rod Heikell has spent more than 40 years sailing and writing about the Mediterranean, in the progress amassing an extensive collection of papers and books on the history of yachting in the Mediterranean and participating in the modern era of that history. In this book he has painstakingly put together the history of sailing for pleasure in the Mediterranean from the ancient Egyptians up to the present.

Beginning with the royal yachts of the pharaohs, the book looks at the Greeks and the influence of the Odyssey, the excesses of Caligula and the poems of Catullus, the scant history of the Middle Ages and the Renaissance, the Romantic poets, and Shelley's sad demise on his yacht. It explores the French writers and artists who sailed these waters, the Victorians and Americans who toured the Mediterranean in their yachts, up to and through the 20th century. The social and political upheavals of the last century changed the world and gave the impetus for many to escape the woes of a post-war world and sail down to the azure waters and warmth of the Mediterranean. Despite recessions and the age of austerity the numbers of yachts has exploded in the 21st century. The book is illustrated with numerous photos and illustrations from the author's collection and other sources. The book is for those who mess about in boats and those with an interest in the history of the Mediterranean, as well as being a reference for more serious research, with extensive reference footnotes.

Anyone who has been sailing in the Mediterranean for any length of time will know all about Rod Heikell's guides. They are absolutely invaluable and a fine example of where you can't really beat having a good solid physical book to browse through. Although Heikell has done guides for all corners of the globe, he started out in the Mediterranean – and it's fairly clear that this is his first love. With that in mind, there can be few better qualified to put together a history of yachting in the Mediterranean. Heikell starts with the very roots of leisure sailing, describing Shelley and Byron's misadventures off La Spezia, and then goes on to narrate some of the more venturesome voyages that have been undertaken on this magical sea. It's clear that the Mediterranean is Heikell's passion and therefore the book is authoritative while also retaining an easy entertaining style that often shines through when an author is writing for pleasure on a subject they know inside out. The book is more than just a look at sailors: it explores the Mediterranean itself, looking at weather, navigation and destinations, interwoven with the story of what is surely a sea with the richest and most diverse history of them all. It makes for a great read. *Sailing Today*

Full colour hardback ISBN 978-0-9954699-5-2   Price £32.50 Also in Kindle.

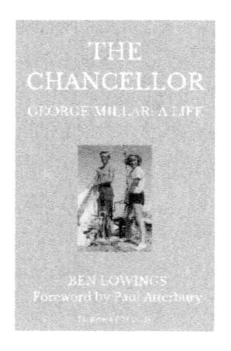

THE CHANCELLOR
George Millar: A Life
Ben Lowings

CHANCELLOR was the code name Britain's Special Operations Executive used for one heroic agent fighting behind enemy lines in France during the dark days of 1944. This is the first biography of him, the 'sailing Scotsman': George Reid Millar, DSO MC (1910-2005).

It is fair to say George loved water. He rowed for his university, worked his passage to the Pacific as a steamer's deckhand and searched for a liner's sunken treasure off Ireland. On a reporting job, he got a scoop on the Wallis Simpson story by breakfasting aboard the royal yacht with King Edward VIII.

He joined the army after a spell in the Daily Express Paris bureau, and got captured in Libya. Two breakouts failed and he found himself inside Germany. An amazing escape followed. He then parachuted back into Nazi-held France and fought with the Resistance.

The war over, the memoirs a publishing success, Millar – with his new wife - voyaged into a Mediterranean Sea which was reopening to foreigners again. This book reveals that George carried a secret cargo aboard their yacht, Truant.

Unpublished novels, hitherto private correspondence and archive material tell the tale of a brilliant man of letters, a talented boatman and equestrian, whose work has been latterly neglected.

Ben Lowings is a London-based journalist and yacht delivery skipper, who wrote a life story of the New Zealand sailor and explorer, David Lewis (The Dolphin, Lodestar Books, 2020).

BY THE EDGE OF THE SEA: Essays and semi-true tales after 50 years on the Sea

In Kindle and Epub. Paperback POD from Amazon £13.95.

Over the 50 odd years Rod Heikell has been living on and sailing boats around various bits of the world he has accumulated a little bundle of stories and reflected on the places he has been to and the people who live there. And he has reflected on how he arrived in no direct way on the peripatetic path he has taken. It's easy to construct a biography on hindsight, but these are inevitably flawed, nay false, stories, told to make it look like we took a path on some perfect logic when in truth there was something of an accident about taking that path. A variant of the Dunning-Kruger effect.

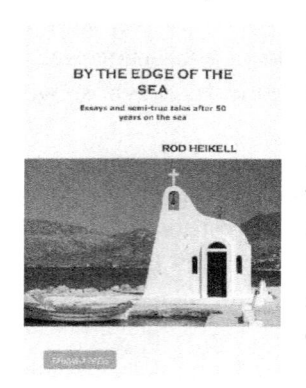

Most of the essays and semi-true stories here are new, though some have been published elsewhere or are extracts from some of the other books I have written. Some are semi-true to protect the guilty and the innocent and in one I have changed the location, but the bones of the stories are true. Most of the essays and stories are based in the Mediterranean where he has spent most of his time sailing around its shores, but there are a few other edges of the sea from scattered parts of the world.

However you read this I hope it measures out a little salt water on your life and gives you a measure of the life around the edges of the sea.

Title   By the Edge of the Sea

Sub-title Essays and semi-true tales after 50 years on the sea

1st edition 2020

ISBN 978-0-9954699-8-3

The Mapmaker's Shadow

Two men separated by five centuries and yet inextricably linked by a map.

Ricard Hogarth is a respected professor at Durham specialising in the history of cartography and in particular early Turkish maps and the charts and portolans of Piri Reis. He has risen through the ranks from his working class roots to be an internationally renowned scholar. And yet he is not really comfortable in the academic milieu he has landed in. His life is turned around when he meets a young Australian post grad student and they fall in love. His life is shattered when his young Australian wife suddenly disappears for no reason he can fathom. A little later he has a catastrophic breakdown in front of his students and leaves the university to live on a boat on the canals in the south of France, an exile by choice in a place where no one knows where he is or of his past life. Until he is tracked down by an enigmatic young man to validate a lost map by Piri Reis.

Piri Reis has risen through the ranks under his uncle Kemal Reis to become an esteemed captain in the Ottoman navy. But his temperament is not for the blood and gore of battle, and he yearns to be left in peace to draw his maps and work on his Book of the Sea. Somehow, he has to navigate his way through the intrigues and wiles of the Ottoman court without losing his head as sultans come and go. To his dismay the viziers keep sending him off on naval missions when he would rather be in his study in Gelibolu at the top of the Dardanelles.

This book interweaves the life of Ricard and the life of Piri Reis five centuries earlier. They are not the same men but both are caught up in a life not entirely of their own making. Somehow the fabric of their lives is intertwined, their hopes and loves have an affinity, and though the outcome of their lives is separated by circumstance and time, we can see the parallels despite the centuries between them.

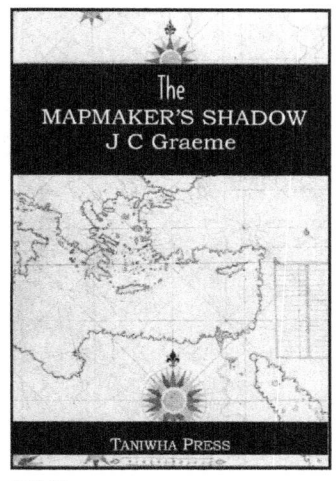

ISBN

978-1-7397072-0-0
In Kindle and Epub. POD from Amazon £8.95

Printed in Great Britain
by Amazon